MW01265079

HOLLY JOLLY TALES!

Kids Christmas Short Story Collection for Age 5 & Up

Holly-Anne Divey

ISBN-10: 1480249262
ISBN-13: 978-1480249264

COVER CREDITS -

COVER DESIGN :
Holly & Ivy Books, USA

IMAGES :
Christmas Elements – Rudolph and
Christmas Elements – Santa 2
by fangol (FreeImages.com)

Snowflake Photoshop Brushes &
Chrismtas Vectors by ObsidianDawn.com

FONT :
Candy Randy by Lauren Ashpole (DaFont.com)
Komika Display by Vigilante Typeface Corporation
(DaFont.com)

ACKNOWLEDGEMENT:
'A Hollywood Christmas Carol' is a derivative work of
'A Christmas Carol' by Charles Dickens, which is
now in the Public Domain.

'A Hollywood Christmas Carol' is my tribute to
Dickens and his Christmas masterpiece which
is very, very dear to me, and always plays
a huge part in my Christmas, every year.

TABLE OF CONTENTS -

ALL I WANT FOR CHRISTMAS
IS A PUMPKIN!

Bobby was obsessed with Halloween.

All year round he would look forward to it – the dressing up as some scary monster, carving pumpkin Jack O' Lanterns, all the candy and other gruesome goodies like spider rings and plastic vampire fangs.

He loved Christmas too, and birthdays, of course, because of all the presents. But to Bobby, Halloween was the awesomest holiday.

But all too soon everybody would forget all about his beloved Halloween. The day after everybody would take down their fake cobwebs and Styrofoam gravestones and shut them away for another year. And they'd put up fall decorations right away; the cartoon turkeys and the cutesy scarecrows with smiling faces.

Blech! I hate those goofy things! Bobby would think to himself when they went up on November 1st. Even his mom would put up an orange-yuck fall wreath with fake leaves and plastic acorns on it. He hated that too.

And he would have to put up with all this fall stuff and Thanksgiving stuff that was just not cool, until Christmas came around and he could have some awesome decorations again.

On Halloween night, after munching on way too much candy, he would try to stay up for as long as he could to make Halloween last as long as possible, because he knew he would not see it again for another whole year.

A few days after Halloween, Mom would make Bobby throw away his Jack o' Lantern. It would start to turn black and smell like burnt turnips and furry mold would appear around the cut edges and inside, making the pumpkin look like it was growing hair.

He would be so sad the next day, watching Mom take down his spooky decorations and shut them away in a big plastic box with a lid. She'd shove them up in the attic so he couldn't even play with them if he wanted. And he would have to wait another 364 days until Halloween came around again.

It was so boring and horrible waiting for Christmas to arrive. He knew he would have to eat a pile of turkey and stuffing before it got here, and be sick and tired of eating turkey sandwiches for a week after Thanksgiving.

And he would have to look at that yucky orange wreath thing on the front door every time he went out it or came in it, for nearly two whole months.

To keep himself occupied while he longed for Halloween to come back, he would think about Christmas instead, and look forward to all the presents he knew he would get.

He knew he would have to kiss and hug a bunch of people he didn't really know, like old ladies with beards and hair that moved who Mom called her *aunts* and *cousins*. He would have to kiss and hug them all over again at Christmas, but that wasn't so bad, because they always brought tons of presents and goodies to eat with them during the holidays.

The day after Halloween was particularly oogie for Bobby. He sat at the table playing with his cereal until the milk was warm and it looked like a mushy mess.

"Bobby, what's the matter?" Mom asked him, frowning with worry.

"Nothing," Bobby said, totally lying.

"Come on, sweetie. I know when there's something up. You've been my little man for ten years now, buddy," she said. All moms know that – they can just tell when something is wrong with you.

"It's just the day after Halloween. You know it makes me sad," he said.

"I know, Bobby. But there's always next year. And, you know, if it was every day, it wouldn't be so special, would it? Just like Christmas. We would end up thinking Christmas was blah if it came around every week, wouldn't we?" Mom said.

"I guess so," he said, still sulking into the gloopy mess in his cereal bowl.

"Hey, what do you want for Christmas this year?" Mom asked, trying to take his mind of Halloween being over for another year.

"All I want for Christmas is a pumpkin!" he said.

"A pumpkin? I don't know if we can get a pumpkin around Christmas, sweetie. Not one big enough to make a Jack o' Lantern out of. Probably only be a able to get the tiny little ones for making pies with, like a *Jack Be Little* or a *Sugar Pie.* " Mom said.

"That's what I thought. Oh, well. Never mind," he said, and sighed dramatically, picked up his lunch box and his rucksack and headed out the door for the school bus.

* * *

Bobby counted down the days until Christmas. The closer it got the more excited and restless he became. Mom even caught him rummaging around in the hall closet trying to hunt down Christmas presents she'd hidden. He denied that was what he was doing – he said he was just looking for the Halloween decorations to play with. But he knew they were in the attic, like they always were, so he wasn't fooling anybody.

"Why would you want to spoil the surprise on Christmas morning, Bobby?" Mom asked.

"I just wanted to know there was something to look forward to, that's all," he said.

"Don't you *always* get a whole bunch of cool stuff at Christmas? Have you ever been disappointed with your presents?" Mom asked.

"Yes I do. And no I haven't," he said, answering both her questions, hoping he got the answers in the right order.

"And you just lied to me, Bobby," Mom said, looking at him with a sad face.

"I'm sorry, Mom. I didn't mean to upset you," Bobby said.

"Stop looking for presents. And don't lie to me, OK?" she said.

"OK," he said, walking off with his head down, feeling ashamed now for lying to his mom.

Mom had given him a totally awesome Halloween party this year and he realized that he didn't even enjoy himself, because he was too busy thinking about the next day and Halloween being over. He was thinking about it so much that he forgot to have a good time at the cool party his mom spent weeks organizing for him.

Now he was sad that he had upset his mom and he had lied to her, and he had wasted the whole party she worked so hard on sulking about Halloween only being for one day a year and that it would be over too soon.

"I'm a big doofus," he said to himself.

"No, you're not," Mom said from behind him.

"Mom, I'm really sorry. I was a pain yesterday. I want you to know that it was an awesome party and I really appreciate it. Thank you, Mom," he said, going to her and giving her a big hug.

"You're welcome, sweetie," Mom said, smiling, and kissed the top of his head with his mussed up hair he'd forgotten to brush that morning.

* * *

Finally, it was Christmas!

Just like he always did, every Christmas morning, he flew down the stairs in his pajamas yelling *Merry Christmas*! and ran around the living room three times in a circle.

Mom and Dad were laughing at him – it was always funny, no matter how many times he did it.

"Oh, boy! Look at all those presents!" Bobby said.

"What do you want to open first? How about this one?" Mom asked, picking up a huge present that was so big it didn't fit under the Christmas tree.

"I saw this and I had to get it for you," she said, smiling already, before he even opened it, because she knew he would go nuts when he saw it.

Bobby started by tearing the ribbons and big Christmas bow off, then ripped into the paper.

He gasped when he saw what it was.

"Oh, my gosh! A giant pumpkin! A giant pumpkin!" he yelled, and took off for another lap around the living room, running in circles again, totally loving his present.

It was a giant artificial Jack o' Lantern with a big grin and scary eye holes. There was a light bulb inside it and it plugged into the power outlet and lit up brightly.

"I saw it in the store, the day after Halloween. And you said all you wanted for Christmas was a pumpkin, So, there it is!" Mom said.

Bobby was still jumping up and down and ran to his mom and gave her a huge hug.

"Thanks, Mom! Thanks, Dad! I can't believe you found this!" he said.

Bobby got his Christmas wish, to get a pumpkin on Christmas Day. And he realized too, that not only did he get what he wanted for Christmas, but he had a totally awesome Mom too.

THE PERFECTEST CHRISTMAS TREE
IN THE WHOLE WIDE WORLD!

Penny is a fuss-pot. She's a perfect *Little Miss* and has a neat and tidy bedroom where nothing is ever out of place. Everything is pink and pretty and it's the perfectest bedroom in the whole wide world. She doesn't even play with her toys very much, because she doesn't like to make a mess and muss up her neat and tidy room.

Penny's mom is the same. She's a fuss-pot too. Their house is like one of those you see on the TV and everybody who visits is scared to even sit down on the couch in case they mess it up.

Every Christmas Eve Penny and her mom go to town to get their Christmas Tree. But it has to be the perfect Christmas tree, of course, to go with their perfect house. Nothing but the best will do for Penny's mom.

* * *

Penny was starting to get tired and a little bit grumpy and she didn't really feel perfect anymore. Penny and her mom had been running around Christmas tree lots for hours and hours. All day they'd been to this lot and that lot and the other lot and the lot around the corner and the one across the road looking for the perfect Christmas tree. She was sure she would dream about Christmas tree lots tonight, she had seen so much of them today.

"Oh, Penny; these trees are just not good enough!" Mom said. "It's almost three o'clock. We have to get a tree soon or we're not going to have time to decorate it before dinner. We have guests coming! If I have to rush it will be far from perfect!"

"What about this one, mommy?" Penny asked, pointing to a Christmas tree that she thought might be pretty close to perfect.

Penny thought to herself – *it's tall and bushy – Mom likes that. It's simmy...semmie...what was that word again, the one that means the left side looks the same as the right side? SYMMETRICAL! Yes! That's it! This one is symmetrical. Mommy likes that too – a symmetrical Christmas tree.*

But Penny's mom didn't think that it was perfect. She said that it leaned to one side, that the trunk was a bit squiffy and lop sided.

Penny didn't really see that at all. She thought it was fine. But mommy didn't think it was perfect so she didn't buy it. Penny liked it, though. She thought it was an awesome Christmas tree.

So, they went around *all* the tree lots again and just as they arrived at each one, the owner sold the last tree that they had in stock.

The whole town was selling out of Christmas trees!

It was Christmas Eve and Penny wasn't going to have a tree to trim for the Holidays and thinking about it made her want to cry. Decorating the Christmas tree was one of Penny's favorite parts of the Holidays. She had such fun and would wrap herself up in tinsel and roll around on the floor which would make her mom nervous about the mess she might make with it, but it would make her laugh too. And the tinsel would make Penny sneeze when little bits of it tickled the end of her nose.

Penny and her mom would put on fun Christmas songs and drink hot chocolate with melty marshmallows in it while they were decorating the tree. Penny loved looking through all the baubles and deciding which ones to put on. There were boxes and boxes of them, far too many to use all of them every time they decorated the tree.

While they were putting up the decorations inside, Dad would be outside the house hanging up the Christmas lights in the front yard, and putting the big huge Santa in his sleigh on the roof, and making sure he had his reindeer – all 9 of them.

Penny would always be too excited to fall asleep on Christmas Eve, so Mom told her to try and remember the names of all Santa's reindeer. Usually she couldn't remember them all – or at least not all at the saFme time.

She would lie awake, pulling the curtain open a little and keep an eye on the sky, just in case Santa passed by and she could catch a glimpse of him.

She'd start counting the reindeer and trying to remember all their names – counting them off on her fingers as she remembered them...

1 – Rudolph – he's the one who lights up the night sky to guide Santa's sleigh with his shiny red nose.

2 – Donner

3 – Blitzen

Grandma would read her *The Night Before Christmas* every Christmas night before she went to bed. She told Penny that *Donner & Blitzen* meant *Thunder & Lightning* in German.

4 – Dasher

5 – Dancer

6 – Prancer

7 – Vixen
8 – Comet
9 – Cupid

But right now, they still had no Christmas tree and it just wasn't going to be the same if they had to have Christmas without one. And even counting Santa's reindeer wouldn't help her to sleep tonight if she knew there would be no Christmas tree to take her presents from under on Christmas morning. It just wouldn't be the same.

Penny was sad as each tree lot they went back to was closing, all the trees sold out, and the owners were about to return home to their own families for the Holidays, and decorate their own Christmas trees.

Penny wished Mom had bought one of the other trees earlier. Even a tree that wasn't completely perfect would be better than no tree at all.

Mom saw Penny's said little face and wished she had bought one of the less than perfect trees too. She was also sad they weren't going to have a tree – she loved decorating the tree with Penny every year, and dancing around to fun holiday songs and drinking hot chocolate with gooey marshmallows in.

Penny tried not to look too sad on the way home in the car. She didn't want her mommy to feel bad about not buying a tree, but she couldn't help looking a little bit glum.

They got home and unloaded all the bags of presents and goodies and treats into the house when Penny heard Dad's truck pulling into the drive.

Mom heard Penny squealing and ran outside to see what was going on.

"A Christmas tree! Daddy! You got a Christmas tree!" Penny yelled loud enough for the whole street to hear.

Dad laughed.

"I sure did, sweetie! I wasn't going to leave it up to Mom – I was afraid they would be all be sold out before she found one she liked!" he said. "I thought, if you guys came home with one and we ended up with two, then we could just put it out front and throw some lights on it and have one in the front yard too."

Dad hauled the Christmas tree from the truck bed and into the house, set it in the stand that was already lying there that Mom had put out before they left for town that morning.

"Oh, daddy! It's the perfectest Christmas tree in the whole wide world!" Penny squealed.

"It *is* perfect," Penny's mom said. And she realized that what was most fun and most important the her about the Christmas tree wasn't just the tree itself, but spending time with Penny decorating it, and dancing and being goofy, and drinking hot chocolate with gooey marshmallows in.

AUNT GINNY'S CRUDTASTIC
CHRISTMAS SWEATERS

Every Christmas Aunt Ginny came to visit for a whole week, sometimes longer. She wasn't much older than Johnathan's mom, and she wasn't *really* her Aunt at all.

Johnathan hated it when she came to stay. He curled his lip.

"Christmas Eve again. She'll be here soon," he sighed

He was the one who had to give up his bedroom for her to snore in. *He* was the one who had to toss and turn for seven nights, sometimes longer, on an uncomfortable old camp bed.

He was the one who always got some lame, crudtastic Christmas sweater with Scotty dogs wearing tartan jackets or penguins with Santa hats, or something just as yuck. Sometimes it even came with ugly-pugly wooly Holiday socks that were too thick to wear with any of his shoes.

Johnathan was sure, 100%, that this year would be no different from all the other years. He sighed again.

He was getting older now. Thirteen. He wasn't going to be seen dead in one more pair of wooly socks with candy canes on them, not one more sweater with jingle-bells and bows on it.

"Never again!" he cried out in his room.

He shuddered as he wondered what on earth his Christmas sweater was going to look like this year.

And then suddenly he felt bad.

Aunt Ginny's so sweet. She loves me like I was her own nephew. I shouldn't be so ungrateful Johnathan thought to himself.

And then he remembered something from a long time ago, something he'd not thought about since he was a little boy. It was something he had completely forgotten about until right now.

When Johnathan was seven years old, his mom went into hospital to have his baby sister, Virginia. It was just a couple of weeks before Christmas.

That same day, Johnathan got terribly sick with a flu bug. He remembered his mom not being there, and his dad running around like a headless chicken and always rushing in and out.

Who had looked after him while he was sick, who had come to stay and nurse him back to health and stroked his hair while he threw up everywhere, and stayed up late and read to him when he couldn't sleep for feeling oogie?

"Aunt Ginny! Oh, my glob! It was her!"

And then he laughed. It was Aunt Ginny who told him to say *oh my glob!* instead of doing what she called *taking the Lord's name in vain.*

He remembered her spoon-feeding him her yummy homemade chicken noodle soup. And the way she would squeeze fresh oranges and lemons, heat up the juice and add runny honey to soothe his scratchy throat, and give him a dose of Vitamin C. He still loved that hot drink. Now he knew why.

Johnathan was always pretty mean and moody with Aunt Ginny when she gave him another one of her handmade crudtastic Christmas sweaters.

She always looked so thrilled with herself when he opened up the present and mumbled "Thanks, Aunt Ginny," as if the three words hurt his mouth to say them.

And then Johnathan remembered something else. That Christmas when he was just getting over being so sick and Mom and Dad were fussing over the new baby, was the first Christmas Aunt Ginny gave him a Holiday sweater.

And it all came back to him. He remembered everything.

Johnathan was curled up on the couch under a snuggly blanket, sipping one of Aunt Ginny's special hot drinks. They were watching some old Christmas movie. A kid came on screen wearing a Holiday sweater.

Johnathan sighed.

"What's the matter, sweetheart?" Aunt Ginny asked.

"I wish I had a cool holiday sweater," he said, pouting.

"We'll, we'll just have to wait and see what Santa brings you. Won't be long now - just a few more sleeps. But you have to get all better before Christmas comes, or you won't be able to go out and play in the snow. You don't want to be cooped up in your room for the whole Holidays, do you?" Aunt Ginny said, knowing that he was fine now and just enjoying being looked after so well.

"I feel a lot better now," he said. The last thing he wanted was to miss Christmas. It was his favorite time of the year. Even better than birthdays. But it wasn't *just* all the presents he got that made him love Christmas.

Mom and Dad always have a huge party on Christmas Eve and everybody comes. There were friends and family from out of town, even some who now lived in other countries, and all the neighbors in the whole street would be there. The house would be jam packed and everybody who came brought some little gift with them. Johnathan got to open every one of them, so it was like getting a hundred extra presents, even if some of them were Holiday paper plates with matching napkins that he didn't have any use for.

Dad would always do a spectacular Christmas yard display that brought people from all over town to see it.

And Christmas Eve was when Aunt Ginny would arrive too.

Aunt Ginny smiled at him, knowing how much he loved the Holidays. She wondered if she could have a sweater done in time for Christmas morning. She thought she could, since she was a expert knitter.

The warmth of the snugly blanket and the soothing hot juice had made Johnathan nod off to sleep. She found some paper and a pencil and started to sketch out an idea for Johnathan's first Christmas sweater.

When he opened his present from Aunt Ginny on Christmas morning, Johnathan's face lit up and he bounced around the living room with glee when he saw what it was.

He jumped up and down like he had springs on his feet, screaming "It's a Christmas sweater! It's a Christmas sweater!"

Johnathan realized something now – Aunt Ginny giving him that first Christmas sweater, and every one after it, was because she loved him dearly. And they reminded her of that special time they spent together, just the two of them.

She made all the sweaters with her own hands – designed them and knitted them, hand sewed tiny little decorations onto them.

Each time she gave him a Christmas sweater, she hoped that it would make him feel the way he did when she gave him the very first one all those Christmases ago.

"What's that thing Mom always calls me again? Oh, yeah – *ingrate.*" Johnathan asked and answered himself. "And she's right. That's *exactly* what I am."

And he *had* been ungrateful, most definitely. He knew it. He'd been mean and rude at times too, to a lady who loved him like he was her own son.

Johnathan decided that he had some growing up to do. He realized that sometimes you have to do something you don't really want to do for somebody you love.

17

"Yeah, that's what they call *sacrifice* – when you do something for somebody else and don't think about yourself," he said to his empty room.

This Christmas – he'd made up his mind – he would make sure Aunt Ginny saw how much he loved his new sweater, no matter how crudtastic it was.

He'd even decided that if the sweater came with matching wooly socks again, he would wear them and run around the house with no shoes on if he had to.

* * *

It was Christmas Eve and Aunt Ginny was due to arrive at any moment. Dad and Virginia had left to pick her up ages ago.

"Johnathan, why do you keep peeking out the window?" his mom asked.

"Oh, nothing. Just looking forward to seeing Aunt Ginny," he said.

She looked at him as if he had two heads and one of them had boogers running out its nose.

"I love Aunt Ginny. Why wouldn't I be looking forward to seeing her again?" he asked.

Mom put the back of her hand to his forehead.

"Well, you don't have a fever, so what's this all about?" Mom asked.

"I just remembered some stuff I'd forgotten, that's all," he answered.

Mom smiled. She knew what he meant; she'd heard him talking to himself in his room earlier.

Johnathan finished trimming the tree and put the last bauble on a branch.

He stuffed the Christmas decoration boxes back into the hall closet, standing on his tip-toes to stack the last one.

Mom opened the front door to hang the beautiful Holiday wreath she had decorated with scented pine cones and a big red velvet ribbon.

"Aunt Ginny!" Mom cried.

"Penny, darling! Merry Christmas!"

"Merry Christmas! Come on in, it's freezing out there."

"Aunt Ginny!" Johnathan hollered and launched himself down the hall at her and into her arms.

"Sweetheart!" she giggled at such a welcome, delighted and shocked.

"Aunt Ginny, I love you!" Johnathan said.

"My goodness! I love you too, honey," she replied.

Johnathan hugged her until his arms hurt from squeezing.

"Merry Christmas, Aunt Ginny," he said.

"Merry Christmas, Johnathan."

Aunt Ginny sat down on the basket chair in the hall. Johnathan parked himself on the stairs. She knew he had something to say.

"I'm sorry," he said.

"Whatever for?" Aunt Ginny asked him.

"I've been really mean to you for a long time and made you think I don't love you. I'm just a butt-face," he said.

Aunt Ginny laughed.

"No, you're not, silly! It's me who should be sorry for making you wear my crudtastic Christmas sweaters year after year!"

Johnathan looked at her, shocked, eyes wide.

"You *knew* I called them that?" he asked.

"Yes. Who d'you think taught you that word? It was me!"

Johnathan laughed. He had forgotten Aunt Ginny was so funny and goofy.

"Hey, grab that box on the doorstep and put it under the tree while me and your mom grab the other presents, would you?"

Johnathan opened the front door and saw the box sitting on the path.

"Oh, my glob; it's huge! What is it?" he asked as he struggled to move it inside the house.

"Can't tell you – it's a surprise. I *can* tell you what it isn't, though – it's *not* a Christmas sweater!" Aunt Ginny said, and laughed.

"It's for me?" Johnathan asked, doubtful.

"Yep. But no peeking and trying to peel the paper off and stick it back together again before morning, because I'll know, got it?" Aunt Ginny said, winking at him. She remembered he used to do that all the time when he was a little kid.

"I won't! I promise!" he said, laughing.

Johnathan couldn't imagine what on earth was in the box.

*Got to be something totally awesome! h*e thought, still fighting with the huge gift.

He finally managed to wrestle the box into the living room and placed it as near the tree as he could. It was way too big to go underneath and there were already tons of presents under there.

Aunt Ginny and Mom came back from the car lugging a gigantic bag that was so big it took both of them to carry it. It seemed like some sort of magic bag – the presents just kept coming and it took ages to empty all the presents and place them under the tree.

Johnathan smiled at Mom and Aunt Ginny. He was one happy kid.

All three of them looked out the window at Dad and Virginia finishing the light display in the yard. Then the most wonderful thing happened.

It started snowing. Big, thick, heavy white flakes began to fall from the sky, quickly turning Dad and Virginia's hair and shoulders white as the light outside began to fade.

And suddenly the yard came to life with bright lights as Dad plugged in the power cords. Virginia was jumping around with delight as the display blazed to life and lit up Christmas Eve.

Mom, Aunt Ginny and Johnathan went outside in the snow to get a good look at Dad's new display of Christmas lights. The yard and the front of the house, all the trees and bushes, the fence – everything, was covered with tiny, sparkling white lights, thousands of them all glittering in the gathering darkness.

A few of the neighbors started to wandered over to have a look too and awe at the beautiful display.

Johnathan smiled at his family, looked up at the sky and smiled at that too.

Johnathan knew that this was going to be the best Christmas ever.

DEAR SANTA, ALL I WANT FOR CHRISTMAS
IS A TALKING SNOWMAN! LOVE...TIMMY

Timmy couldn't sleep. He never could on Christmas Eve – he was just too excited, what with Santa coming tonight and everything. And they might even get a white Christmas this year too.

He'd heard his mom and dad talking about the weather report as he was climbing the stairs to go to bed.

Massive snowstorms...

Record snowfall...

All-time low temperatures...

Two feet of snow expected...

Were some of the things he heard Mom and Dad and the people on the TV say.

"Two feet! That's a *lot* of snow!" he said excitedly, but quietly, as he climbed the stairs to his room.

All night Timmy kept waking up, kneeling on his bed below the window and peeking out the curtains, watching and waiting for the promised snow to start.

He got up for the fifth or sixth time, looked out the window and sucked in a shocked breath – it was snowing!

He opened the window then went to his desk and took a ruler out of his pen pot and stuck it in the snow to measure how much had fallen so far.

"Three inches already!" he said loudly, then clamped his hand over his mouth for being so loud in the middle of the night.

Everything was so pretty outside, covered in a thick blanket of crisp, white snow for as far as the eye could see.

All the trees in the front yard were white and frozen, and not a single blade of grass nor a patch of green could be seen in the fields that surrounded the house. He smiled as he looked out into the bright night.

Timmy always got what he wanted from Santa, but this year he would understand if he couldn't bring him what he wanted. It was very unusual and he didn't even know if such a thing existed in the whole wide world.

He'd written his letter to Santa early this year – in September – and didn't tell anybody about it. He just addressed it to Santa, North Pole, got a stamp, and put it in the mailbox. He wanted to make sure that Santa had plenty of time to find one for him, just in case they were extremely rare, which he thought they probably were.

Dear Santa,

All I want for christmas is a talking snowman. That is all. I don't know if you can get one or not but if you can't get one then it is OK I will not be mad or anything. If you can't get me a talking snowman then anything else will do I do not mind one bit what it is. Thank you Santa! Love...Timmy.

He knew it wasn't normal for a snowman to talk, but Santa was magical and if anybody could get him one it would be him, he figured. Santa got around the entire world in the one night on flying reindeer and visited every single boy and girl on the planet. If he could do *that*, then he could probably do just about anything.

After kneeling on his bed watching the snow fall faster and deeper for a while, Timmy decided he'd better get some sleep; if he stayed up much longer he might sleep all the way through Christmas and miss out on presents and snow and everything. He didn't want that to happen.

Timmy fell asleep holding the ruler in his hand, dripping melted snow all over his pillow.

* * *

For the first time in all of his six years, Mom and Dad had to wake him up on Christmas morning.

"Merry Christmas!" Mom and Dad yelled as they burst into his room.

Timmy rubbed his eyes sleepily and yawned. Then he realized what day it was and sprang out of bed, quick as a flash.

"Merry Christmas!" Timmy said to his parents.

"You stayed up half the night looking for snow, didn't you?" Mom asked with a grin.

"Some," he said, grinning back at her. There was no point in lying to Mom – she *always* knew when he wasn't telling the truth. He didn't know how she did that but she did it all the time.

"Let's go see what Santa brought you," Dad said, and they all rushed downstairs.

Mom flung open the living room curtains so they could see how much snow had fallen overnight. Everything was covered in white and at least a foot of snow had fallen. It must have snowed the whole night after Timmy saw it begin to fall.

"Hey, what's that in the front yard?" Mom asked.

Timmy gasped in surprise.

"It's my snowman!" he yelled, jumping up and down with excitement. "Can I go outside and see him, can I, can I, pleeeeeeeeeeease?" begged Timmy.

"Make sure you bundle up good – it must be freezing out there!" Mom called after him as he flew out the living room door and into the hall, already putting his snuggly jacket and hat and scarf on.

Timmy raced outside into the front yard to see his snowman, his Christmas present from Santa.

* * *

He was an awesome snowman. He wore a tall black Top Hat with a sprig of fresh holly and bright red berries sitting on the brim, and a huge, cozy red and white striped wooly scarf around his neck. He had huge blue eyes that sparkled and a bright orange carrot for a nose. His mouth looked like it was made from a line of raisins shaped into a smile.

"Oh, my gosh! My snowman! Hi, snowman! I'm Timmy," he said.

"Hi, Timmy! I'm Snowy!" the snowman replied.

Timmy gasped.

"You *do* exist!" Timmy squealed and threw his arms around the snowman to give him a big huge hug.

"I sure do, Timmy! Santa said you've been a very, very good boy this year," Snowy the Snowman said.

"Yeah, I have! I did really good in school and everything. Where do you come from, Snowy?" Timmy asked.

"I'm from the North Pole, where Santa's Christmas Town is. That's where we make the toys for all the girls and boys," Snowy said.

"What's it like there?" Timmy asked.

"It's cold!" the snowman said.

Timmy laughed at his goofy snowman.

"Must be lots of fun having snow all the time, huh?" asked Timmy.

"Oh, it is! In Christmas Town every day is Christmas and every day we have snow and you can have snowball fights or build a snowman, like me!" Snowy said.

"Wow! I would love to live there with snow every single day!" Timmy said.

Mom and Dad were watching Timmy out the living room window.

"Did you get up in the middle of the night and build that snowman?" Mom asked Dad with a grin.

"No, I didn't. I thought you did," Dad replied.

"*Me*? I wouldn't go outside in the middle of the night, on my own, in a blizzard and build a snowman!" she said.

"Oh," Dad said.

"D'you think he snuck out and built it himself?" Mom asked.

"I don't know. I think he would know not to do that. He's a sensible kid. And look at that thing – it's so perfect. See how round the big snowballs are that he's made from. And look at they way he sparkles. He doesn't look he's made from the same snow that's on the ground. It's weird," Dad said.

"I think he's a beautiful snowman, whoever made him," Mom said.

"Maybe it was Santa!" Dad said, with a chuckle.

"I don't know where Timmy would get a Top Hat like that, or the scarf. We don't have either of those in the house. Not even anything like them," Mom said.

"Beats me, honey," Dad said.

They were both puzzled by the perfect snowman turning up in their front yard and they kept on talking about it while they watched Timmy out the window chattering to his new frosty friend.

Mom opened the window and called out to Timmy.

"Timmy! Time to open presents, sweetie!" Mom hollered.

"Coming, Mom! I have to go now, Snowy, but I'll be back soon," Timmy said to his snowman.

"Ta-ta for now, Timmy!" Snowy said with a smile.

"See ya later!" Timmy said and ran off back into the house.

Timmy kicked off his rubber boots and hung up his jacket and wooly scarf and hat, and joined Mom and Dad in the living room.

The house was lovely and warm after being out in the freezing cold. Mom was putting all the presents into piles for each of them. There was a big pile on the coffee table for Timmy.

"Wow! Is all that for me?" asked Timmy.

"Sure is. You've been a good kid this year. And you're *definitely* on Santa's *Nice List*!" Mom said.

Timmy smiled at Mom and Dad and said thank you as he sat down and began tearing open the gift wrap on his presents.

Timmy kept looking out the window at his snowman, just to make sure he was still there and hadn't run off somewhere.

Once they were done with opening presents, Mom told Timmy to go get showered and dressed, then he could go back outside and play in the snow.

He raced upstairs, got showered, threw on his clothes and dried his hair in six minutes flat! He raced back down the stairs and rushed outside again. Dad followed Timmy out there.

"So, did you get what you wanted from Santa?" Dad asked.

"Yep," said Timmy with a smile.

"What did you ask him for?" asked Dad.

"I asked for a...um...I asked for a snowman," Timmy said.

"A snowman? Why would you ask Santa for a snowman? We build a snowman every year, sometimes more than one," Dad said.

Timmy chewed his lip and thought for a second, wondering whether or not to tell Dad that his snowman talks – he was afraid Dad would think he was strange. He figured there was no way Dad would believe him.

"He's a *special* snowman, Dad," Timmy said, finally.

"I know he's a very nice snowman, but what's so *special* about him?" Dad asked.

Timmy still wasn't sure whether to tell Dad about Snowy or not. But he didn't have to.

"I can talk!" blurted Snowy before Timmy could make up his mind.

Dad let out a little scream of surprise and looked at the snowman, his eyes big and his mouth open in shock.

"I told you he was special!" Timmy said.

"I don't believe it. This is...this is...incredible! A *talking* snowman!" Dad said excitedly.

"Hi, Mr Thompson; I'm Snowy!" the snowman said, introducing himself to Timmy's dad with a smile.

"Umm. Hello, Snowy," Dad said, wondering if he was maybe still asleep and dreaming about a talking snowman.

"I asked Santa for a talking snowman this year, Dad. And I got him! He brought me Snowy. I sent my letter to Santa early this year but I didn't tell anybody. I thought he might need some extra time to find my present. I didn't know if they were real or not, but they are!" Timmy said.

"I guess so," Dad said, scratching his head, trying to figure all this out. He thought he might be on some TV show that played tricks on you and looked all around him.

Mom was feeling left out after spending some time alone preparing food in the kitchen, so she joined Dad and Timmy in the front yard for a break.

"Hey, you guys; what you up to?" Mom asked.

"Honey, you're not gonna believe this..." Dad said.

"Believe what?" Mom asked.

Dad and Timmy looked at each other, knowing Mom was going to scream when she found out about Snowy. They didn't know how to tell her. So Snowy helped them out again.

"I can talk!" Snowy blurted again.

Mom screamed.

And Snowy screamed, scared by Mom.

"It's OK! Calm down!" Dad said.

"Don't be scared, Mom. Snowy's a friendly snowman," Timmy reassured his mom.

"But...how?" she said, staring in awe at Snowy.

"He's my present from Santa, Mom. Isn't he awesome?" Timmy said.

Mom started laughing.

"I get it, you guys! Very funny!" Mom said.

"What do you mean, honey?" asked Dad.

"Well, obviously you two thought you'd play a Christmas prank on Mom. Good one! You had me fooled there for a second," Mom said.

"We're not fooling, Mom. Snowy's real. Honest!" Timmy said.

"Oh, now, Timmy – you got me, OK? That's enough now," Mom said.

Dad chewed on his lip. He had a feeling that Mom would never believe them, no matter what they said. He wasn't sure he believed it himself!

"Ha ha! Got ya! It's freezing out here, let's go back inside, honey," Dad said to Mom.

"But Dad!" Timmy yelled.

Dad just looked at him and shook his head, and Timmy knew that meant no to say anything more.

Timmy just smiled. He didn't care if Mom didn't believe in Snowy the Talking Snowman Santa had brought him for Christmas. He knew Snowy was real, even if she didn't.

Timmy stayed outside to play with his snowman while Mom and Dad went back inside the house.

"How did you do it?" Mom asked Dad.

"How did I do what?" he asked.

"How did you make that snowman?" she questioned.

"Oh, you know – it's technical," he said.

She looked at him, waiting for a little more detail than that.

"I looked it up online," he said.

"Really? I don't think so," Mom said.

"What do you mean?" Dad asked, knowing she didn't believe him.

"Well, you need Timmy to show you how to use your cell phone every time you want to listen to your voice mail! And you expect me to believe *you* made a *talking* snowman!" Mom said.

"OK, OK. I didn't make the snowman," he said.

"Then who did?" Mom asked.

"I don't know...Santa?" Dad said.

"Maybe it was my dad. Or maybe it was *your* dad. Either of them could do it. They're both pretty good with electronics. Unlike somebody I could mention!" Mom said, poking Dad gently in the tummy. "Maybe I should call them both before everybody leaves to head over here."

"No! Don't do that!" Dad said, in a bit of a panic.

"Why not?" Mom asked him.

"Timmy didn't tell anybody what he asked Santa for this Christmas. Except Santa," Dad said.

Mom was totally confused now. Dad seemed to be telling the truth, but how could it be? Snowmen don't talk! Do they?

Mom put back on her coat and went outside again. Timmy was laughing and clowning around with his new frosty friend.

Mom stood in front of Snowy with her hands on her hips. Timmy thought she looked like she was about to yell at Snowy. She was determined to find the truth about this mysterious snowman.

"OK, Snowy the Snowman; where did you come from?" Mom asked.

"I'm from the North Pole," Snowy told her.

"What's 2 + 3?" she asked.

"5," answered Snowy with a giggle.

"Who's the president of the United States?" she asked the snowman.

"Barack Obama. He's a Democrat, you know?" Snowy said.

Now she was even more confused. The voice of Snowy the

Snowman was definitely not just some sort of recording. He was really answering her questions!

But there *could* be somebody hiding somewhere and listening, answering for the snowman.

Snowy started to giggle as Mom stuck her hand into one of his snowballs and rummaged around, looking for a speaker or some other electronic thingy.

"That tickles!" Snowy said through his laughter.

There was nothing inside him – except snow. And where she had stuck her hand in and scooped out some of his snow, it began to fill up again, magically, before their eyes.

Her mouth fell open at the sight. She stared at Timmy, then at Dad who just came back outside, and then at the special, magic snowman.

"Well, I guess this means snowmen really *do* talk!" she said.

Suddenly, she took off running, scooping up a handful of snow as she went.

"Snowball fight!" Mom yelled.

Piles of perfectly round snowballs appeared all over the front yard for them to throw.

Timmy threw one at Snowy and knocked his elegant Top Hat right off his head and into the snow!

"Good shot, Timmy!" said Snowy.

Timmy picked up the snowman's hat and put it back on his chilly head.

Mom and Dad were laughing and throwing snowballs at each other and at Timmy and his snowman.

Suddenly, hundreds of snowballs began floating through the air and softly hit Mom and Dad and Timmy and they all laughed.

There was Christmas magic all around them as the snow began to fall again. Timmy smiled and hugged his snowman as they watched Mom and Dad playing in the snow.

"You're my favorite Christmas present ever, Snowy. And this is the best Christmas ever!" Timmy said.

Snowy the Snowman chuckled.

"Just you wait until next year, Timmy – I'm coming back with some friends!"

A HOLLYWOOD CHRISTMAS CAROL

"Merry Christmas, Ms. Rouge!" said Rob Pratchett enthusiastically as he came in the front door.

Lizabetta Rouge mumbled some undecipherable insult at him as she passed by.

He greeted her the same way every Christmas Eve, wishing the old curmudgeon all the best for the Holidays.

Rob adored Christmas with his family and not even the crotchety old Ms. Rouge could extinguish his Christmas spirit. It burned brightly in his heart and it was *the* holiday of holidays for him. It was a time for celebration, a time for the family, a time to be thankful for what we have, no matter how difficult the past year has been. That was Rob's Christmas philosophy and he'd lived by it his entire life.

"Will you be spending Christmas with your niece this year? Nicole's a lovely girl," Rob asked, knowing the answer but always hopeful that she would change her mind, just one year, and spend the festive season with her relatives, and share some Christmas cheer with them.

"Of course not, you foolish man. What would I do a thing like that for? The only reason they invite me is because they expect *me* to spend *my* hard-earned fortune on lavishing presents for them," she said, as if the thought of spending *any* money on anybody made her ill.

"Oh, I don't think that's true, Ms Rouge. Nicole adores you," Rob said. And he was right – Nicole *did* adore her, although he couldn't imagine why, most of the time.

Every year Nicole came to the mansion and invited Ms Rouge to her own humble home, almost apologetic for the lack of glamor in her own life. Every year her aunt said something mean. *Every* year. But she kept coming back each Christmas, without fail.

Car headlights illuminated the gathering darkness, momentarily banishing the long shadows that crept along the great entrance hall of the mansion.

"That'll be Nicole now, Ms Rouge. It would do you the world of good to spend some time with your family over the Holidays," Rob said.

"Humbug!" Ms Rouge growled at him as the doorbell rang. She gestured impatiently for Rob to open the door.

"Oh! Merry Christmas, Rob!" Nicole said.

"Merry Christmas, Nicole!"

They hugged each other warmly and as Nicole handed Rob a Christmas card for him and his family, he looked like she'd handed him a sack full of gold.

It was all extremely tiresome for Ms Rouge who stood rolling her eyes at their Christmas spirit.

Both Nicole and Rob wished it would snow in Hollywood on Christmas Eve, just once.

"Aunt Lizabetta! Merry Christmas!" she said.

"Nothing merry about it...except all the drunks who'll be littering the streets after dark," said Ms Rouge.

"Aunt Lizabetta, please come and spend Christmas with us this year. We'd love to have you. Big party tonight with all the family and friends and neighbors, and tomorrow, it's usually just us and the kids. We just had our third baby, two months ago. We'd love it if you would get to know the kids," Nicole said, ever hopeful but never really sure why she bothered with her. She guessed it was the link to her own mother who had died young in a tragic accident. She had been an actress too, just like Ms Rouge. And for some reason, she *still* loved her Aunt.

Her sister had always outshone her on the stage and on the screen and it was only after her death that Ms Rouge really shone and blossomed into a fine actress, finally stepping out from her sister's shadow.

Their rivalry had been fierce. It was legendary in Hollywood. Harley Rouge cared about nothing outside her career. She didn't care about her own daughter who grew up waiting backstage in theaters and in the dressing rooms and trailers on movie sets.

Although she was ignored by her mother, she remembered those days with happy nostalgia when her Aunt Lizabetta would talk to her and tell her stories, tell her she would always look after her, no matter what.

Ms Rouge had forgotten all about those days. And she had forgotten all about the little girl that she once loved so dearly. Over the years, Ms Rouge had turned her own heart into a cold, hard stone.

"Good grief; *another* child?" she said in a tone dripping with accusation.

Nicole just smiled. Nothing on earth could possibly crush her Christmas cheer.

"Well, the invitation is there. You're very welcome. The party starts tonight at 8:30, and on Christmas Day, we eat around 3 o'clock. I hope you come Aunt Lizabetta," Nicole said.

"Don't hold your breath, girlie," Ms Rouge said, turning form her niece and flouncing haughtily through the archway and into her sumptuously decorated sitting room. The only reason it was decorated that way, though, was because she paid nothing for the furnishings. She squeezed them out of the poor man she bought the house from, a man who gambled his entire fortune on funding a movie that flopped at the box office. He was desperate and Ms. Rouge used his dire situation to her advantage to take him for all she could get.

Ms. Rouge was mean all round – mean of spirit and mean of purse.

And she *always* gets her own way.

Nicole knew it was a waste of time to come here every Christmas, but she did anyway. And she would keep coming back, every year, no matter how many times Aunt Lizabetta refused her invitation and stood there scolding her for her kindness and her simple joy in Christmas.

"Well, the invitation stands, as always. I love you, Aunt Zabby," she said.

Nicole thought she saw the slightest hesitation in Lizabetta's step when she called her *Aunt Zabby.*

That was Nicole's name for her when she was a little girl. She couldn't say *Lizabetta,* and it came out as *Zabby.*

She hadn't thought of it for years but it came back to her as she searched her mind for some way to get through to her, some way to convince her to change her mind and come back to the arms of her family.

There was nothing more that she could say. She wondered if she should maybe just give up now, just move on and forget about Aunt Lizabetta. Perhaps she should just stop doing this to herself every year and just let it go.

Nicole said her goodbyes to Rob Pratchett and to her Aunt's back and returned to her husband in the car.

"I don't know why you bother with her, honey," David said.

"Because she's my Aunt and I love her," she told him.

"What is there to love? She's never said a kind word or visited in all the years we've know each other, Nic."

"I know, I know. I should quit. I know I shouldn't care, but I do. Don't ask me not to," she said.

"I wouldn't do that, sweetheart," he said.

"I know," Nicole told him.

She smiled sadly at him in the soft darkness of twilight as they began heading home to spend a happy evening with family and friends at their annual Christmas Eve party.

* * *

"Ms. Rouge?" Rob said.

"What is it, Pratchett?" she asked, testily.

"I was wondering if you need me any more today?" he asked.

She looked at the clock on the mantle.

"It's only 6:15pm, Pratchett; you don't finish work until seven. Is there something particular about today that you should need to leave early?" she asked him.

"Um, I guess not, except it's Christmas Eve. Aren't you going to your niece's Christmas party this evening?" he asked her.

"You know the answer to that, Pratchett. Why on earth would I take part in nonsense like a Christmas party?" she tutted and rolled her eyes at him, as if he'd said something utterly outrageous.

"Because she's family and she loves you," Rob said.

"Pratchett, do you like your job?" she asked.

"Yes, of course," he lied.

"Then it would be of benefit to you to shut your mouth and keep your nose out of my personal life if you want to keep working for me," she snapped at him.

And he did. He shut his mouth. He couldn't lose this job. He needed it. It was getting expensive looking after Little Jim, and Marlena would have to give up work; Rob didn't think Little Jim would be able to go back to school after the Holidays.

"Yes, I thought so," she said, her face smug now as she looked down her nose at him. They looked at each other in silence for a moment. Rob remained quiet, even although there were a thousand things he wanted to say to her right now, and most of them not pleasant.

He wanted to tell her she was a miserable, joyless, miserly old woman who will die alone and nobody, except one person in the whole world would care.

He wanted to tell her that there was no reason for her to live her life this way, and that there was a family – her family – waiting for her, right now, to celebrate Christmas together.

But he did not. He stayed silent, for the sake of his *own* family.

"Off you go, then. You're no use to me full of all that *Christmas Spirit* and *Joy to the World* nonsense. Humbug! Just be here at eight on the nose the day after Christmas, you hear me?" she asked him.

"Yes, Ms Rouge! Thank you! Merry Christmas!" Rob called out to her, grabbing his jacket and fleeing, before she changed her mind.

"No better than a thief, robbing me because of a holiday every 25th of December and getting paid for doing no work. Scandalous!" she yelled at the echoing interior of her silent, darkening house.

* * *

"Daddy!" yelled Little Jim Pratchett, the apple of his father's eye.

The fragile little boy threw himself into his dad's arms.

"Merry Christmas Eve, Daddy!"

"Merry Christmas Eve, LJ!" Rob said, smiling from ear to ear.

Then his smile faded from his face as his son slumped and hung limp in his arms like a soft rag doll.

"Poor thing," Marlena Pratchett said, kissing her husband on the cheek and gently picking up her little boy. "He's been so excited he wore himself out. I think he's getting worse, Rob," she said.

"Oh, don't say that," Rob said, shaking his head in denial.

"I mean it, Rob. He can't even go to school anymore. I'm not sending him back after the Holidays. He's just too sick."

Rob's face hung slack, his shoulders slumping downward in defeat. He knew that Little Jim was getting worse by the day, but he just couldn't face the thought.

"I just wish we knew what was wrong with him. We're getting nowhere with doctors. All they do is scratch their heads and send us bills," she said.

Rob looked at her blankly. He didn't know what to say. But she was right. It had been five years since Little Jim had first taken ill just short of his second birthday, and they were still no closer to an actual diagnosis.

The poor kid had been poked and prodded, stuck in huge machines and stabbed with needles for too long now. And it was all in vain. They still didn't know what was wrong with him. One Doctor even had the nerve to tell her Little Jim was faking it.

She was tired of watching what was once a vibrant, robust, whirlwind of a child fade away, wither and almost die.

No mother should have to watch her eight year old son hobble around with a cane like a little old man.

And she was angry. She wanted to take Little Jim to a Naturopath, since all else had failed him so far. But the insurance company wouldn't hear of it. They refused to pay even part. And her son continued to get worse, became sicker and sicker, week after week.

So, now, the Holidays were here again and Little Jim was one step closer to his last Christmas. Marlena Pratchett succumbed to the tears and anguish she seldom allowed herself to indulge in. She was on the brink of letting go of the last shred of hope she clung to.

Rob stood in the shower, radio up loud so Marlena and the kids couldn't hear him cry.

He knew his wife carried most of the burden and would be the one who the other kids asked the most difficult questions. He didn't want her to have to humor and comfort him too.

What are we gonna do? Why can't they help him? How can so many Doctors fail to help a sick little boy? Why don't they know what's wrong with him? God, please help us. I know we need a miracle, but, please, please, don't let my little boy die.

Marlena could hear Rob crying in the bathroom. She knew he thought the radio drowned out the sound. It didn't. She could always hear him. Sometimes she could hear him praying to, begging God to make Little Jim well so he could go back to being a normal kid again and live a full and happy life.

Rob sat down at the kitchen table and ate a late dinner. Marlena sat down across from him. His mask was slipping and he knew it. The strain showed on his face and he looked so much older than a man only in his thirties.

"You don't have to put a brave face on all the time, you know," Marlena said.

He looked at her, still trying to control his sorrow but failed miserably. Hot tears spilled down his face as his wife came to him and cradled his head in her arms as he wept.

Her own tears fell silently down her cheeks.

Even the idea of hoping for a miracle seemed like a cruel joke to both of them right now.

* * *

"You know, that old bag ruins Christmas for you every year, because every year you expect her to show up. And all you do is curtain twitch, look out the window and watch the clock. She's not come one single time, sweetheart. She's never going to," David said.

"Don't talk about her like that. She wasn't always this way, you know. She *will* come one year. I know she will," Nicole said.

"Well, don't hold your breath, Nic," he said.

David despised the old woman for the way she treated Nicole. But he was also annoyed with his wife for going back to her each year for more punishment. He just didn't understand it.

The doorbell rang and Nicole rushed to it leaving David standing there shaking his head at her.

It's Aunt Zabby! It's her! I knew she would come!

She smiled in anticipation of opening the door and seeing Lizabetta standing there, finally come to spend Christmas where she belonged - with her family.

She hid her disappointment well from the guests at the door; it was David's co-workers from the movie studio where he was in charge of Security.

She was so disappointed but then felt guilty as she thought about poor Rob Pratchett and his family spending what might be their last Christmas with their sick little boy.

She looked over at her own children – happy, healthy, robust, and without a care in the world. She couldn't even imagine how Rob and his wife could function. She knew she would fall to pieces if if one of her own children was seriously ill.

Maybe Aunt Lizabetta never would come for Christmas, but that was her own choice. At least she had her kids, a wonderful husband and all of them had their health.

Suddenly she felt wretched as she realized she had forgotten to do something earlier.

Oh, my gosh. I didn't even ask him how Little Jim was doing.

She decided that after the Holidays she would make a point to drop by the mansion for a cup of coffee and a chat with Rob.

* * *

Ms Rouge made her way up the creaking stairs of her lonely old house. She looked about her; long dark shadows seemed to chase her up to her bedroom door on the top floor. She hurried inside and locked the door.

She made a meager fire in the fireplace, much too mean and tight-fisted with her vast fortune to heat the whole house, even for her own comfort.

She'd brought up with her half a can of cheap, store-brand soup for dinner, with half a slice of dry, stale bread. She was too miserly to even feed herself properly.

She slurped at the modern-day gruel then set it down on the nightstand with a *tut* as she heard a group of carol singers outside the house.

"Stop that infernal racket! You sound like strangled cats!" Ms Rouge screamed from the bedroom window upstairs in the mansion as she flung it open violently.

She was incensed that they had dared to make their way down her drive. She supposed the bright red bucket one of them was carrying meant they wanted money too.

"Merry Christmas, Ms Rouge!" yelled a rosy faced carol singer.

"Humbug! Get off my property before I have you all arrested," she yelled down at them.

The carol singers didn't protest; they just kept right on singing and turned around, made their way back down the long drive.

"The nerve! Screeching like that in the middle of the night. Humbug!"

She slammed the window closed.

It was chilly; she felt a draft creeping in under her bedroom door and nipping at her ankles as she crossed the room to get into bed and finish her soup.

"Shouldn't be this cold in California; feels like Siberia in here. Ridiculous," she said to herself, but she still wouldn't turn on the heating.

The house, even in California with its mild winters could get chilly at this time of year. But tonight, the brick seemed to radiate an icy chill, much worse than she had ever felt. As her teeth chattered her hot breath was visible in the cold air around her. She pulled her worn old blankets up around her chin.

It didn't take long for the book she was reading *Maximizing Your Investments : From Millionaire to Billionaire* to bore her to sleep and slide to the floor out of her hand.

* * *

"Lizabeeeeetta," said the soft, breathy whisper that filtered through the darkness.

Ms Rouge stirred in her sleep, her eyes fluttering rapidly.

"Lizabeeeeetta," the voice said again, louder this time.

Her eyes opened and she screamed as she looked into the pale face of her long-dead sister.

Lizabetta sprang out of bed like a six year old on Christmas morning and ran around the room, screaming and waving her arms.

"Oh, Lizzy; do calm down, darling," Harley said. "Stop being such a drama queen."

She rolled her eyes at her sister. Lizabetta could make a drama out of anything, she remembered.

Lizabetta stopped in her tracks and stared at the specter of her sister standing before her.

"B...b...but...you...you're..."

"Dead? Yes. Quite," Harley said.

"But how can this be happening?" Lizabetta asked, slack-jawed and staring at her sister's ghost.

"How should I know? I don't make the rules. I just knew that I needed to come back and give somebody I love a good talking to," Harley said.

Lizabetta stared blankly at her.

"You, you idiot!" Harley yelled at her, exasperated.

"Oh," she replied. She paused for a moment, trying to regain her normal grumpy composure. "What on earth are you doing creeping around in the middle of the night scaring people half to death anyway?" She frowned at her sister's ghost, the stony facade returning.

"I told you, I came to help you mend you ways before it's too late," Harley said.

"Mend my ways? I'm perfectly fine. I don't need to *mend* anything," Lizabetta said.

"Do you see this?" Harley asked, pointing to the miles and miles of film stock, movie cameras, metal film cans and hundreds of framed pictures of herself that were attached to a long, heavy gold chain she wore around her wrists, waist and ankles. The attached items floated around her in the air, dragged behind her on the floor. She looked like a bizarre Christmas tree. Loose publicity shots or her and magazine feature pages swirled around the room.

"Yes, I was wondering what *that* was all about. I thought it might be the latest fashion in the hereafter," Lizabetta said.

"Still sarcastic, I see," Harley said.

"It's all part of my charm," she replied.

"That's one thing you're not, Lizzy dear – *charming*. You couldn't charm a snake. These things that surround me and I will carry around for all eternity are the burdens I made for my soul throughout my life. *This* was all I cared about. My image on the screen, my box office receipts, which gossip rag was talking about me. And let me tell you, sis, none of the things I cared about have been any comfort to me over here. I threw my own daughter's love away for the falseness of the hangers-on around me, the ones who told me how brilliant I was, how beautiful I was, told me how much everybody in the whole world loved me. But none of them actually cared about me. My own personal assistant robbed my safe only hours after that falling lighting rig killed me on set."

Lizabetta looked shocked.

"Oh, my God; is *that* how he managed to finance the movie that made him a fortune; he stole it from you?"

"Yes. That's how he did it, the little rat. Now he's one of the top producers in Hollywood, has one of the biggest houses in Laurel Canyon and a new trophy wife that's young enough to be his grand-daughter. Anyway, enough chit-chat. Time is short. I don't have long. I came to tell you something. It's Christmas Eve and there's a girl waiting for you who loves you very much, waiting for you across town. There's a family who needs an aunt to love and cherish them. But I don't expect you to just take my word for it. You probably don't even believe your own eyes, do you?" Harley said.

"No, I don't. You're probably a side-effect of the MSG in the soup I ate for dinner, or the dough conditioners in my bread," Lizabetta said, trying to convince herself the presence of her dead sister was nothing more than an hallucination.

"Well, believe in me or not, suit yourself. But you might be convinced by the others that will visit you tonight. Three of them. Take heed of what they say, sis. I have to go now. I love you."

An icy gale blew through the room and a blizzard of glossy photographs of Harley swirled in the air. Then the wind was gone and the pictures floated slowly downward and landed at Lizabetta's feet.

She shook her head, still not convinced what she had seen was actually real. She climbed back into bed, pulled the covers up over her head and tried to forget about it.

She tossed and turned, scrunching her eyelids shut tight, pulling the covers up over her head. Despite the chill in the room she had a sheen of sweat covering her brow. Sleep would not come to her.

She didn't know how long she had been lying there, restless, sleepless, when she threw off the covers and decided to get up.

She screamed as she saw a man standing in her room, smiling at her.

"Hush. Don't be afraid of me, Lizabetta. I wish you no harm. In fact, the only person who brings harm to your door is yourself. That is why I am here," the man said.

"Who are you?" she cried out, hugging one of the four posts around her bed as if the wood offered her some comfort or protection.

"I'm the Ghost of Christmas Past," the man said, still smiling.

"Are you an angel? Am I dead`? Did I die in my sleep?" she asked, her alarm growing.

"An angel? I guess I am. Sort of. But no, you're not dead," the man reassured her.

Her fear subsided a little as he reassured her that she had not died in her bed, and she became fascinated by him. His skin seemed to glow in the darkness of her room and his eyes shone with light and sparks from within. He was dressed in white gossamer clothing that was sewn with a golden thread, and had long white hair that gently danced around him.

"What do you want with me? Why is my dead sister visiting me in the middle of the night, for pity's sake?" she asked him, her fear tightened throat making her usually deep voice sound shrill.

"I have come to show you the things that you have forgotten. To show you the kind, loving woman you once was and can be again. And your sister came to tell you I would be coming, and that the others would be coming too. Harley loved you in life and she loves you in death. And she regrets not being a better sister. She has eternity to regret. She doesn't want you to suffer the same fate," the spirit said.

"Humbug," Lizabetta said defiantly. "I don't believe in ghosts. I must have a dose of the flu, or something. I'm clearly hallucinating. I'm going back to bed now to sleep it off. And when I wake up in the morning, I'll realize this was all some insane fever dream."

The ghost reached out to her.

"Then you have nothing to lose nor fear by taking my hand and letting me take you on a journey to Christmas Past, do you?"

"I guess not," she said, shrugged and took the spirit's hand.

And in a heartbeat they were flying through the air, soaring in the chill night sky above Los Angeles, looking down on the city below, and the Hollywood sign which looked tiny, like a miniature model, they were so far above everything.

And then suddenly they were on the ground and Ms Rouge found herself smiling broadly as she instantly recognized the place they now stood, from her childhood so long ago.

"Oh! Oh! Look! We're at the *Hollywood Stardom School for Girls*! I went here. And my sister, Harley. We were both very popular, you know?" she boasted to the Ghost of Christmas Past.

"Wasn't Harley much more popular than you were, Lizabetta?"

Ms Rouge shot him a look.

"I know everything. Lying to me is only lying to yourself. I know what you know about your own life, and perhaps some things you would rather not remember," the spirit said.

"So what if she was more popular than me? I was *still* popular. She was *always* better at *everything*. She was always more talented than me. She was always prettier than me. And blah, blah, blah," she said, her mood instantly reverting back to her norm, all trace of her smile and pleasure at seeing the old place gone now.

"You were *both* happy here. This was before the sibling rivalry and your jealousy poisoned your relationship with her. This was a time that was carefree and innocent."

"Yes, we were happy here. These were the happiest times of our whole lives before...before... *everything,*" Ms Rouge said.

"You mean before your jealousies made you what you are today?" the spirit asked, bluntly.

Ms Rouge gave the Spirit of Christmas Past an evil look.

"The way I am didn't come easy. Do you think it was fun always being in her shadow? You think I enjoyed always being second best, when I worked so hard, even harder than she did, and I never got the attention she did? I didn't get the recognition I deserved until after she was gone. But even then my fame was a sham. It was although I was some sort of replacement for her audience, a substitute Harley. Do you think that felt good? Do you think that made my life wonderful, always walking one step behind a woman who was the nation's darling? Do you?" Ms Rouge's voice got louder and louder as she ranted at the spirit.

"There's no need to shout – I'm right here. All I'm doing is showing you how things were. Don't shoot the messenger,

Lizabetta."

The room spun for a second and Ms Rouge found herself standing in the theater of the stage school, looking up at herself under the spotlights, her audience captivated by her performance in the play – until the stunning Harley entered Stage Left and extinguished her sisters light.

Something changed in Lizabetta at that moment. Standing there, looking back at it, spectating the moment her whole life changed, she could see a light going out in her own eyes. She could see defeat, see her own shoulders slump as she slowly back-stepped off stage.

She ran through the crowd of people backstage and into the bathroom where she began to cry hysterically.

Ms Rouge and the spirit were now by young Lizabetta's side watching as she was defeated, watching as she quickly became bitter, right before her own eyes. Tears quivered in her eyes and quickly spilled down her face, unable to hold them back. She was just nine years old.

"Why didn't you go back on that stage and out-shine *her?* Why did you just give up? You didn't even try, Lizabetta. Why?" the spirit asked.

"Because she had *always* outshone me. Even as *babies* doing commercials, *she* was the one everybody used to go gaga over. This day – on this stage - was just the day I knew I would never be able to beat her at anything," Lizabetta said, her voice soft but carrying no emotion, flat, monotone.

She sighed and looked suddenly weary. The spirit shook his head sadly, knowing that Lizabetta had not been defeated by Harley, but by herself.

"You know, I've lived my entire life being introduced as *her* sister. Spent my whole career being interviewed about what it's like to be *her* sister. I loved her. I still love her. But the way people treated me, the way they praised her and worshiped her, well, it made me hate her too," she said, her voice beginning to waver, just a little.

"She loved you dearly, Lizabetta. She still does. Why else would she bother to come back from the dead to try and prevent you from suffering her eternal fate?" the spirit asked Ms Rouge.

"I don't know why she would bother. I don't know how she could love me. I don't know how anybody could ever have loved me," she said.

"You weren't always the person you are now. You were once a loving, happy, caring sister and daughter. Harley and your parents adored you. But then again, they *always* adored you, no matter how you treated them. And Nicole loves you too, no matter how horrid you are to her every time she comes to see you, no matter how rude you are to her when she comes to invite you to her home to celebrate the Holidays with her family, every Christmas Eve, without fail," the spirit said, studying Ms Rouge's face, searching for a reaction to her words.

"I want to go home now, please. Take me home!" Ms Rouge demanded of the spirit.

"Oh, I 'm not done with you yet, Lizabetta. I have more to show you. Come with me."

Ms Rouge sighed and followed the spirit.

In a heartbeat they were in another place, another time and watching Ms Rouge on another Christmas Eve.

"Oh, my God! Harley's wedding! We're at Harley's wedding. It was on a Christmas Eve. Everything was..." her voice trailed off. She didn't say how perfect it was, or how beautiful it was, because all she could actually remember about that night was her own behavior.

"Go on, Lizabetta; what was it?" the spirit coaxed.

"Nothing," Ms Rouge said and cleared her throat.

"What's the matter?" the spirit asked.

"I said nothing," she replied, snappily.

"Are you remembering how you tried to sabotage your sister's wedding? Do you remember how you acted that day? Can you remember how you felt that day, the things that went through your mind, all the rage and hatred that coursed through you because of your jealousies?" the spirit inquired.

They were both silent as they stood and watched a replay of the day and snippets of the days prior. Ms Rouge had tried various things to ruin Harley's wedding – calling the florist and changing the color of the flowers so that they would clash with the Bridesmaids dresses, changing the menu for the reception to include horrid, disgusting dishes, including chocolate covered insects and tripe, breaking a stink bomb at the front door of the church. All childish, juvenile tricks and pranks that she had been ashamed of for a lifetime.

Ms Rouge sank to her knees, buried her head in her hands and wept for the shame of it all.

When she pulled herself together she was kneeling on her bed, back home in her bedroom, her face still wet with her tears.

She looked around her as she sobbed and wiped her eyes; there was no sign of the Ghost of Christmas Past. She was all alone. Again.

She lay down and wondered if there was something wrong with her or perhaps it had all been some insane dream. She pinched herself, made sure that she was really, really awake and not still asleep, not still dreaming.

She got up and opened the window and shivered as a gust of chill air hit her in the face.

"Well, I'm definitely awake," she said to herself and her room.

"Hello, Lizabetta!" a loud and jolly voice boomed out from the other side of the room. Ms Rouge screamed and spun around.

"You're not dreaming, or hallucinating and neither do you have some strange brain disease. This is as real as it gets. He walked over to her and pinched her hard on the arm.

"Ouch!" she yelled at him, frowning. "What was that for?"

"Just to make sure you know you're awake," the spirit said.

"Who are you? What do you want?" she asked, shaking.

"Can't you guess who I am?" the spirit asked her.

She narrowed her eyes and thought for a moment.

"The Ghost of Christmas Present?"

"Bingo! You *are* clever, aren't you?" he said with a wink.

She wasn't amused in the slightest.

He was like an elegant Santa Claus, with long, flowing locks of wavy white hair tied back in a candy cane striped red and white ribbon, a meticulously trimmed white beard and mustache and an expensive, tailored Santa suit.

"Well, then; what do you want with me?" she asked.

The spirit rolled his eyes.

"I'm going to show you some things happening this very Christmas," the spirit said.

"Oh, joy," she said. "Let's get on with it then."

He winked and smiled at her, crooked his elbow and offered her his arm. She hooked her's through it and the spirit opened the window without touching it and they took off into the chill night air above Hollywood.

"Don't let me fall! I'll be splattered all over the sidewalk!" she cried.

"I won't let you fall, Lizabetta. You're safe with me. Don't you worry," the spirit reassured her.

They stopped at the front door of a modest house, nothing fancy, not too big. A nice, quiet little street. All the houses were lit up with Christmas lights illuminating the darkness.

They watched as an endless stream of people poured into the house – family, friends, neighbors, all bearing gifts and boxes of candy and containers filled with festive party nibbles.

"This is happening right now, Lizabetta. Do you know where we are?" the spirit asked.

"I have no idea. I'm sure I don't know anybody who would live in a street of shoe boxes like this," she said.

"Sure you do. Let's go in. Nobody can hear us or see us," the spirit told her.

The house was decorated with sparkling Christmas decorations everywhere, an artificial tree in the corner that shone with twinkling white lights, it's branches hanging protectively over a pile of beautifully wrapped presents.

She could feel the love and happiness inside this house. All these people were having a great time, stuffing themselves with festive food, dancing to favorite Christmas songs, singing along, out of tune.

And suddenly she felt so alone. So isolated. She was not part of this. She wasn't able to dance with them, or sing with them, she couldn't interact with them.

The spirit heard her thought.

"Why not? You *were* invited," he said.

She looked at him and then realized where she was, just as she spotted her niece across the room.

"Oh, my. This is Nicole's house. I had no idea," she said.

"Well, you wouldn't, would you? You've never been here before...even although she invites you every year, without fail. Even although you always say no, every year," the spirit said, glancing sideways at her.

"She lives *here*?" Ms Rouge asked, unbelieving.

"Yes. Why? Something wrong with it?" the spirit asked.

"Why would she need to live here? My sister was filthy rich."

The spirit rolled his eyes at her.

"Yes, she was...and she left it all to you, remember? To look after her daughter should anything ever happen to her."

"Oh. That's right. She did. But her father took her. What could *I* do? He's filthy rich too. She shouldn't need to live *here*", she said, as if it were some sort of a filthy hovel.

"Remember the man you bought your beautiful house from, you know, the one who lost everything investing in that movie?" the spirit asked her.

"Yes, what about him?"

"Don't you know who his partner was?"

"No, why should I? I didn't know the man I bought the house from. I didn't know anything about him. I didn't care either," she said.

"His partner was Nicole's father, Lizabetta. He lost everything too," the spirit told her.

"Didn't you ever wonder why you didn't see her for so many years after your sister's death? Did you not wonder why she never came to visit you when you two had been so, so close? Didn't you ever bother to find out where she was?"

Lizabetta looked at him with horror all over her face.

"What are you saying?" she asked, afraid of the answer.

"Her father took to drinking after losing his entire fortune – and so soon after his ex-wife's tragic accident. She was taken into protective care and spent the rest of her childhood in foster homes. He's a bum now; you've walked past him dozens of times on Sunset Boulevard, begging for change."

"Oh, my God! You're not serious. I don't believe you. I don't! I don't believe it," she said, shaking her head, denying the truth he was telling her.

"I speak only the truth to you. What reason would I have to lie? I'm here for one reason and one reason only – to help you to change your ways, Lizabetta" he told her.

"Why didn't he come to me and ask for help?" she asked the spirit.

"You ruined his wedding, remember? You hated each other, remember? And your feelings never changed after your sister divorced him. You ever thought of trying Icelandic Krill Oil or Ginko Biloba for that bad memory of yours?" the spirit asked.

"I wouldn't have turned my back on her! I wouldn't! He should have come to me! I would have looked after her! My God in heaven, if only I could turn back time and fix this," she said, her voice trembling with emotion.

"Actually, she was placed with an exceptional family and she grew up to be a wonderful, caring, loving young woman. Not sure she would have turned out the same if you'd brought her up, if you know what I mean," the spirit said.

Ms Rouge sucked in an outraged gasp of air, about to rip into the Ghost of Christmas Present for such an outrageous and offensive comment. But she closed her mouth again and said nothing. Because she knew he was right. If she had brought up the sweet little girl she used to love so much, she would have turned her into a bitter and twisted woman, just like herself.

"You know, if I had been given a chance to take care of her, maybe I wouldn't have turned into what I am. Well, not as bad, anyway. Maybe," Ms Rouge said.

"You started on that path early on, Lizabetta. *Very* early on," the spirit said.

She sighed. She was running out of excuses and justifications for herself. She looked at the spirit, utterly defeated. There was nothing more she could say. Anything she could tell him in justification for her entire life would only be a lie and he would know it.

She watched her niece singing and dancing with her husband and kids to silly Christmas songs and having the best time with such a simple pleasure.

She smiled a sad, sad smile, a smile full of regret as she watched the family she should have been a part of but never was.

"I want to show you something else, Lizabetta. Take my arm again and walk with me," the spirit instructed.

Before she knew it they were standing in a dingy little street in a bad part of town. It was an old apartment building covered in graffiti, its stone grimy and darker than it should have been with the dirt and pollution from the air and the streets of downtown Los Angeles.

"Good grief! How can anybody live here. It's horrible! I couldn't possibly know anybody who lives here," she said.

"That's what you said about the last place. *You* thought *it* was bad. Just look at this place," the spirit said, a look of distaste on his own face.

Miss Rouge screamed as an army of cockroaches ran by her feet.

"What on earth are we doing here?" she asked the spirit, her brow furrowed. She hated bugs.

"You don't know where we are, do you?" he asked.

"Would I be asking what we're doing here if I did?" she asked him back.

The spirit pointed upward to a street sign a few feet above their heads on the edge of the building's facade.

"Oh, no. Oh, no, no, no. This can't be," she said.

"It can. And it is."

"This is Rob Pratchett's place, isn't it?" she asked, closing her eyes, knowing the answer already. She at least remembered his address even if she'd never been on his street before.

"Got it in one! Yes, it's Rob's place. His whole family lives in this two bedroom apartment. Two of the children sleep on camp beds in the living room and have done for years. Another three of them share a tiny room that's not even legally a bedroom. The other child – Little Jim – sleeps in his mom and dad's bedroom. It's horribly cramped. It's in a bad part of town. The whole area is infested with rodents and bugs. But you know what? Considering their situation, the way they hang on to their child's life one day at a time, they wouldn't be any happier with all your money and your opulent mansion, Lizabetta. Because none of that means anything when you face the death of your child coming closer and closer each day," the spirit said, his usually bright, jovial face now serious and somber.

He opened the front door to the apartment and gestured for Ms Rouge to step inside.

There was lots of love and laughter in the apartment's tiny front room with its open-plan kitchen, which was no more than a counter top with a sink, a stove and a refrigerator.

Although the parents – Rob and Marlena – were laughing and smiling along with their children, both of them looked strained, stressed. They looked so much older than in their thirties. Marlena was still beautiful but the constant worry over her sick little boy showed on her face and in the premature gray streak in her hair.

At Christmas they always had a traditional British Christmas Dinner. But it looked like something from the table of a Victorian pauper. The turkey was tiny, the dishes of carrots and Brussel sprouts were sparse, and the small bowl of stuffing didn't seem like it would stretch nearly far enough to feed eight hungry mouths.

"That wouldn't feed a sparrow," Ms Rouge said, looking at the meager spread on their old blue Formica table which was probably older than all their children put together.

"It's all they can afford. They've been ruined by years of medical bills and prescription charges for Little Jim," the spirit told her.

"What *exactly* is it that's wrong with him?" she asked.

"You mean you don't know? You've been Rob's boss for all these years and you two have never talked about his sick son?" the spirit asked, unbelieving.

"Well, he's mentioned him, of course," she said.

"The thing is, Lizabetta, *nobody* knows what's wrong with him. They've never had a diagnosis in all these years and the child, bless him, just gets sicker and sicker and the doctors keep filling him with drugs that make him no better. They've actually stopped all his medications, you know? And he's no better, no worse for it. For now." the spirit said.

"Oh, my God. Oh, spirit, please tell me he's going to be alright. Please tell me he's going to grow up strong and healthy and live a long and happy life. Please!" Ms Rouge cried out to the spirit.

"I don't see Little Jim at any future Christmas gatherings, Lizabetta," the spirit said, his face grim.

She watched the poor little boy try to laugh along with his family, but he barely had enough energy left in his body to pick up a fork-full of food to eat.

Tears streamed down her face as she watched the pale little boy slowly dying with his family around him eating their Christmas Dinner.

"I've had enough! I can't take anymore! What's the point of all this? Why are you torturing me, spirit? Why? Why show me this if it's written in stone and can't be changed? Can I change it? Is there something I can do to make a different future for this poor child?" she pleaded.

"Would there be a point of showing you any of this if there was nothing you could do?" the spirit answered her question with one of his own.

"Then take me back home and let me start to make this better, spirit," she said.

"I can't do that. There is another spirit, as your sister told you, who wants to walk with you on this Christmas Eve."

"Then let's get on with it! I have things to do back in the real world. I've learned my lesson, OK? Point taken!" she said, panic drenching her voice as if her life depended on her getting back to her own space and time and beginning her new existence.

"I must leave you now, Lizabetta. It's almost midnight in your world and so it will soon be Christmas Day," the spirit said, his face warm and glowing now as he said goodbye to her, a friendly smile peeking out from his whiskers.

"Goodbye, Ghost of Christmas Present. Thank you. I mean that," she said, sorry to see him go.

"I know you do, Lizabetta. Goodbye! Farewell! And a Merry Christmas!"

"Merry Christmas!" she called after him as he disappeared into a sparkling snow storm that left a pile of icy glitter on the floor behind him.

She must have been a little girl the last time she wished somebody a *Merry Christmas.*

The sight of the final spirit of the night wiped out all thoughts of the kindly ghost that had just left her. It was unusually tall and clad from head to foot in a black hooded robe. She could see nothing but its flowing cloak, see nothing inside the hood. This one scared her.

"You're the Ghost of Christmas Future, aren't you?" she asked it, her voice vibrating with fear.

It remained silent. Didn't move.

"I'm scared of you," she said.

"Don't be afraid. Just take heed," it said, and held out its arm for her to take.

They stood in the small living room of Rob and Marlena Pratchett. This Christmas there was no tree. There were no presents. There was no laughter nor smiles. Not even a meager Christmas Dinner.

And there was no Little Jim.

"Oh, no. No! Please, spirit! Take me back now! Let me undo this horrible future. Let me help them. Let me help Little Jim and make him better. I'll do anything! I'll even give my life!" she cried out.

The dark spirit's hood snapped around toward her as if her words had shocked it.

"Would you?" it asked.

"Would I what?"

"Would you *really* give you life to save the child this family has lost?" the spirit asked her.

"Yes. Yes, I would. And if it is in your power to take my life and give him back his, then take me now. I'll go willingly," she said. And she meant it.

"Remember, this is a Christmas Day that has not yet been, Lizabetta. But if something doesn't change for this family, if

Little Jim does not get the help he so desperately needs, then this future *will* come to pass," the spirit said.

She buried her face in her hands, no idea how she could help a child that Doctor after Doctor had failed. And she wept, wishing that her life in exchange for his was possible if it meant that he would live and grew up to have a long and wonderful life.

She looked up to talk to the spirit again once she stopped crying.

She was back in her room again.

She gasped.

"I'm alive! The spirits let me live! Oh, my goodness! It's Christmas Day, isn't it?" she asked herself.

She ran around the room like a kid who just found out that Santa had come, even although they didn't *quite* make it onto the *Nice List* this year.

"It is! It is! They've given me another chance. I know I don't deserve it. God knows I don't. I know, I know. But it's wonderful! And I won't waste it! Thank you!" she shouted at the ceiling as if the good spirits from last night were up there looking down on her.

"Oh! There's so much to do! I better get a move on!"

* * *

Once she had showered and dressed in the most festive outfit she could find – a red and white dress that she was surprised she had and was perfect for Christmas Day – she called in a favor from an old friend she hadn't seen in years but knew would not hang up on her when she called.

He was the owner of a department store in town and Ms Rouge ran around the store with two shopping carts filling it with Christmas presents and holiday treats.

She was laughing like a lunatic as she rushed around the store, her old friend barely able to keep up with her, winding himself laughing and running. He'd never seen her like this before.

They stood for an hour wrapping all the presents and she took three bags with her and wrote down an address for him to have the rest delivered to.

"Just bill me for all this. You know I'm good for it. Oh, and, could you be an absolute darling and throw in that beautiful Candy Cane themed Christmas Tree too?" she asked him and he obliged. Of course he would. She rushed off, yelling behind her that they would have to do lunch and catch up with each other. She doubled back.

"And don't tell them where it came from!"

* * *

The department store owner knocked on the door.

"Rob Pratchett?"

"Umm, yes?" he said, wondering what on earth anybody could want knocking on his door on Christmas Day."

"Delivery!" he shouted, laughing at the shock on Rob's face.

"Wait! Stop! There's been a mistake! We didn't order these. We could never afford anything like this!" Rob yelled at the man, afraid he'd be stuck with an enormous bill because of somebody's error.

"They're all paid for, Mr Pratchett! Paid in full. I was instructed to deliver everything to you and your family," he said.

"Who by?"

"Someone who wishes to remain anonymous," he replied.

He didn't know why, or what had happened to her, but somehow, he knew in his heart that the mysterious Secret Santa was Ms Rouge.

He smiled as he watched his children running around screaming at the mountains of gifts and food and the noise increased as the department store owner brought in the beautiful Candy Cane Christmas Tree. It was much too big for the tiny living room but they didn't care. It was no longer going to be an extremely bad Christmas with nothing but a few dollar store toys and hats and scarves for the kiddies, and no Christmas Tree. It was going to be a Christmas filled with hope for a future that none of them could even see before.

Marlena was crying and laughing at the same time, her heart filled with joy at the looks on her children's faces.

And Little Jim looked just like the rest of them for now. It was as if he forgot that he was sick for a few moments, then caught himself, stopped running around and waited to see if he would pass out with the excitement. He didn't, so he started running around and laughing again and for once, Rob and Marlena let him.

"Oh, mommy! Daddy! This is gonna be the bestest Christmas ever!" Little Jim squealed.

And up until then, it was.

Little did they know that from now on, every day would be like Christmas Day.

* * *

Miss Rouge drove past Nicole's door ten times before she asked her driver to stop and let her out and actually plucked up the courage to walk up the path to her little house. Once he'd taken all the bags of Christmas goodies up the path for her, she told him to take the rest of the week off and he sped away before she changed her mind. But he slammed his breaks on and yelled "Thanks, Ms Rouge! Merry Christmas!" out the Limo window.

"Merry Christmas!" she giggled back at him as he screeched off down the road.

Nicole looked out the window to see what all the commotion was and squealed as she saw Lizabetta standing on the doorstep.

"Aunt Zabby!" she screamed and rushed to the front door. Then just stood there, looking at her as if *she* were a ghost.

"Aunt Zabby?" she asked, as if she wasn't quite sure she should believe her own eyes or not.

"NicNic. Oh, my little NicNic. I'v's missed you so much," she said, her eyes filling with tears.

"Oh, Auntie! I've missed you too!" Nicole said and hugged her, all the years of tension and hurt and anger melting away.

"You've come to spend Christmas with us?" Nicole asked, hopefully.

"Yes. If you'll still have me," Lizabetta said, knowing that she didn't deserve a second chance.

"Of course we will! Come on in and meet your family, Aunt Zabby," Nicole said, a beaming smile on her face.

The kids immediately took to her, but she knew that the bags stuffed full of treats and presents probably helped her out.

Even David welcomed her into his home and decided, for Nic's sake, to let the past stay where it was – far, far behind them all.

* * *

Rob snuck through the front door and into his office, quiet as a mouse. He was very late. He hoped Ms Rouge wouldn't notice him sneaking in.

He stopped in his tracks as he heard her screeching his name. "Pratchett! Get in here!"

She scurried into her office, ready to face the music and praying that she wouldn't fire him for being so late when she told him in no uncertain terms *not* to be.

"What time do you call this?" she asked him.

"I'm so sorry, Ms Rouge. Truly. We had an incredible Christmas Day! It was amazing! We had all this stuff delivered from an anonymous person – food and presents for the kids and me and Marlena and this gorgeous Christmas Tree and..."

"This is the end, Pratchett. I've been thinking about letting you go..."

"Oh, no. Ms, Rouge, please. Please don't fire me," he said, trying not to sound like he was begging, but ready to if it was necessary to keep his job.

"But I've decided to give you ten times your salary instead," she said.

He looked at her, sure she was playing some cruel joke on him.

"Excuse me?" he said.

"You heard me – I'm giving you ten times your salary!" she said and burst into fits of laughter.

"Are you alright, Ms Rouge?" he asked, concerned she lost her mind and he might need to call the police.

"I'm more than alright, Rob. I'm so sorry for the way I've treated you all these years. You've been such a loyal employee and you've never complained about how horrible a boss I am," she said. "And what I pay you is just shocking. I've never given you a bonus for the Holidays or for doing such wonderful work for me, never even so much as a *thank you* for putting up with me. I'm sorry and it won't happen again. I owe you this."

"Wow. Uh...thank you, Ms Rouge," he said, stunned and still wondering about her mental faculties.

"And you can call me Lizabetta. We've known each other for years and years and it's time we got to know each other better. And your family. And it's time for that little boy of yours to get well, and as God's my witness, Rob, he will!" she said.

"I don't even know what to say," he said.

"Don't say anything. Let me take you all out for dinner tonight and we'll see what we can start doing for Little Jim, OK? I know people," she said.

Rob's eyes filled with tears and the lump of emotion in his throat wouldn't allow him to speak. There were so many things he wanted to say to her right now, but not one word would issue from his throat.

For the first time in Little Jim's life, Rob Pratchett was filled with hope that it would now be a long and happy one.

"Merry Christmas, Ms Rouge," was all Rob could say.

"Merry Christmas, Rob," said Lizabetta.

And indeed it was.

And so will all their Christmases be, because of a wonderful, kind, generous woman who everybody loved, called Ms Rouge.

CANDY CANES ARE
NOT FOR BREAKFAST!

"Mom! Brad's eating Candy Canes for breakfast again!" Amy hollered at the top of her lungs.

"I'm not eating it for breakfast – it's just an aperitif," Brad told her.

"It's a *pair of teeth?*" Amy asked, confused. She knew her ten year old brother was smart, but she didn't think eating a *pair of teeth* for breakfast was smart at all.

"Not a *pair of teeth – A-PERY-TEEF!*" he said.

"What's that?" Amy asked.

"It's something you eat before a meal to make you hungrier," Brad said.

"Huh?" Amy said, still confused.

"What?" Brad looked at her and he could see his little sister was thinking hard about this.

"What for? Why would you need to make yourself hungrier when you've been asleep all night and not had anything to eat since dinner the night before?"

"How should I know?" Brad said.

And that was the end of it.

Mom came in – she'd been standing halfway down the stairs, listening to them.

"An aperitif is a drink, honey. You know, like a cocktail grown-ups drink," she said.

"Yeah, I know *that,*" he said, rolling his eyes. "But I'm not a grown up yet, so *my* aperitif is candy!" he grinned at his mom.

Mom laughed – Brad was such a hoot. And smart too.

Brad grabbed a banana and an apple for breakfast to eat on the bus to school and slung his backpack over his shoulder.

"Brad! Remember straight home after practice tonight – Danny's mom's picking you up. We're getting the Christmas tree!" Mom said.

"Yay!" Amy said, jumping up and down.

Brad was about to go out the front door when his Mom yelled after him.

"And Brad! Candy Canes are *not* for breakfast!"

* * *

Mandy, whose desk is next to Brad's in class, sat down next to him on the bus.

Brad pulled his Candy Cane from earlier out of his hoodie pocket and stuck it in his mouth. He made a face, pulled it out again and picked off a big ball of lint stuck to the end of it, then started sucking it again.

"You'll rot your teeth, you know?" Mandy said.

"No, I won't," he said.

"Yes, you will. Sugar is bad for your teeth," she told him.

"Well, these are *organic,* so nuh," he said, triumphantly.

"It's *still* sugar!" she said.

"What's with everybody today. Can't a dude eat a Candy Cane in peace any more? I only get them once a year!" he said, his voice loud enough that everybody in the bus started looking at him.

"*Soh-ree,!*" Mandy said.

* * *

The bus route to school went through town; the Christmas decorations this year were new and there were tons of Candy Canes all over the place. Great big lit up ones. Huge wooden cut-out pained ones in bright white and berry red. He smiled at all the different Candy Cane displays.

He opened his lunch box to pull out the banana he grabbed on his way out the door and noticed that Mom had put another mini Candy Cane in his lunch box.

Wo0T! he said inside his head. *Another Candy Cane!*

He loved Candy Canes and couldn't understand why they didn't have other Candy Canes in other colors for other holidays.

Why don't they have black and orange striped ones for Halloween? That would rock! And how about green and white ones for St. Patrick's day – Mom would definitely buy them because grandpa is Irish! That would be awesome! Oh, and we should definitely have Candy Canes in red, white and blue for the Fourth of July. Cooooool, he thought to himself.

As he ran from the school bus and into school, he didn't know if the Candy Cane in his lunch box was going to last until lunch time. He was trying to figure out ways to eat it in class without getting caught.

Maybe I can hold whatever text book we're using on up in front of me like I'm reading it and actually be eating my deliciously awesome Candy Cane behind it. Oh, I know! I could tell Mr Matheson I'm sick with a cold and this Candy Cane is one of those special high Vitamin C pops you get! Awesome! That might work! he thought to himself. He had it all figured out.

Brad sat down at his desk in first period. It was the last day of school before the Holidays and Mr Matheson was busy ordering last minute presents online and told the whole class to take out their math books and do the exercises on page 125.

Yes! Though Brad triumphantly.

Aww, gee. I should have taken it out of the noisy crinkly wrapper before I got into class.

He guessed he hadn't thought it through *quite* as well as he'd figured.

Maybe I can slip in into my sweater pocket and try and poke it through the end of the wrapper. My shirt will make it not so noisy. He might hear me opening my lunch box though. Man! Why didn't I put it in my pocket before I came into class? But maybe he won't notice – I know he's ordering Christmas presents for his family. Hey! He's eating something! I bet he's sneaking Peppermint Candy into his pie-hole when we're not looking!

Brad was mad. They always got in trouble for eating in class. He ducked his head down behind his math book and peeked over the top of it to spy on Mr Matheson. He watched as the teacher looked up, trying to see if anybody was watching him and he popped another Peppermint Candy into his mouth.

I knew it! He's eating Peppermint Candy! He's got some nerve! He's always yelling at us for eating in class. Well, I'm just going to eat my Candy Cane and I don't care what he says! If he tattle-tales on me, then I'll tattle-tale on him too!

Brad looked over at Mandy sitting next to him. Her book was propped up in front of her too and she was eating a Candy Cane!

He looked around the class – all the other kids, some hiding behind text books, some not, were *all* eating Candy Canes and Peppermint Candy. Brad was the only one who wasn't.

He sat up, so mad his cheeks were red - as the red stripe on his beloved Candy Canes. He looked at Mr Matheson.

"Something wrong, Brad?" teacher asked.

Brad looked around him, in disbelief at everybody sitting there eating candy.

"What is it, Brad?"

"Everybody, including you, is eating in class!" he blurted.

"Yes, so?" Mr Matheson asked.

"We're not allowed to eat in class! You gave me detention last month for eating candy!" Brad said, still in disbelief that he was the only person in the class with an empty mouth.

"Well, Brad, let this be a lesson to you to listen to your teacher," Mr Matheson said.

'I...I...do," Brad lied.

"Obviously you don't. If you *had* been listening to me yesterday afternoon and thinking less about getting home to your game console, then you would have heard me telling everybody that today is Christmas Candy Day and you're allowed to eat one piece of Christmas Candy in class," Mr Matheson said.

"Oh," Brad said.

All the kids giggled.

Mr Matheson laughed.

Brad shrugged his shoulders and took his Candy Cane out of his lunch box and popped it into his mouth. "Merry Christmas!" Mr Matheson said, laughing.

"Merry Christmas, Mr Matheson!" all the kids shouted at their teacher and all went back to eating their Candy Canes and Peppermints, and doing the math problems on page 125.

SNOW'S A NO SHOW ON SNOW DAY!

Katie sighed, elbows on the windowsill gazing out at the bare yard.

"It's supposed to *snow* on *Snow* Day," she said, sadly. Life is tough for a six year old when everybody's talking about Snow Day and you've got no snow.

All the city was covered in snow after a huge blizzard overnight. But out there in the countryside where Katie lived on a farm with her mom and dad, there was nothing. Not a single snowflake!

She thought about all the city kids who would be out side playing in the snow right now, bundled up in their bright and cozy hats, scarves and gloves, making snowmen and throwing snowballs at each other.

She sighed again.

"Come on, Katie! We're ready to go!" Mom said from the front door.

Katie put on her coat and got into the truck.

"I wish it would snow," she said, pouting as her dad started the engine.

Mom smiled at her.

"It will, sweetie, don't worry! It'll be all white and frosty and freezing before dark, just you wait and see," Mom said.

"Yep, Mom's right; definitely be snowfall out here before the day's over, honey," Dad reassured her.

"They said on the news they had six inches in the city, overnight," Mom said.

"You think we'll get that much, Daddy?" Katie asked.

"I think we'll get twelve!" he said.

"Twelve inches of snow! Oh, boy!" she squealed, stamping her feet with excitement.

Katie's parents laughed to see her so excited at the thought of snow. She had been so overjoyed when the news declared a Snow Day and she didn't have to go to school. But her excitement didn't last when she ran to the window and flung open her curtains and discovered that there was no snow there at home.

But Mom and Dad both knew that a trip to the tree farm to get their Christmas Tree would cheer her up. And Mom knew that Santa was going to be there this year too.

* * *

"Mommy, look – Santa and Rudolph!" Katie said excitedly as they arrived at the tree farm.

"Oh, wow! Let's go see them," Mom said.

Katie petted Rudolph the Red Nosed Reindeer and gave him a hug. Santa handed Katie a little Christmas present covered in snowmen gift wrap.

"Thank you, Santa!" she said, and tore off the paper. She gasped with delight. "It's a snow globe!" she yelled with glee.

Santa and her mom smiled.

"Thanks, Santa," Mom said and scratched Rudolph's ears.

The little snow globe had a teeny tiny snowman inside, and a pile of snowballs, just ready to throw at somebody. Katie wished she could make herself really, really small for just a short time so she could climb into the snow globe and have a snowball fight with him. Or maybe he could come out of there, grow big for a while and have a snowball fight with her. But they didn't have any snow here just now, so that wouldn't work, she figured.

She shook it up and made a blizzard come down around the snowman inside. She loved it and thanked Santa again, waved to Rudolph and went off with Mom and Dad to pick their Christmas Tree.

"Oooh, look at this one, Mommy," Katie said.

"Wow, pretty. Way too big for our living room, though. Must be ten feet tall," Mom said.

Mom walked around the rows of trees, Katie sometimes behind her, sometimes in front of her. She narrowed her eyes and took a good hard look at all of them.

"Mommy, this is the one!" Katie hollered.

"Where are you sweetheart?" Mom asked, losing sight of her for a second.

"I'm here!" Katie said, peeking from behind the tree she just picked.

Oh, yes. Good choice, Katie! This one's perfect," Mom said, and waved to Dad to come get the tree.

It was thick and bushy and smelled like Christmas. It was an awesome tree.

* * *

Next they headed to town for lunch. Katie and Mom talked about how they were going to decorate the tree this Christmas and that they should make popcorn garlands this year, and collect pine cones from the front yard and paint them white to look like they're covered in snow.

"We can have a Snow Day tree!" Katie said.

"Yes, that's it – a Snow Day tree! What a great idea! Let's do that then, deal?" Mom asked.

"Deal!" exclaimed Katie and shook her mom's outstretched hand.

"Sounds like you guys have a lot of work to do. Why don't you two go on over to Grandma Christmas's store across the street and pick out some new ornaments for your Snow Day tree? I need a few things around town. I'll meet you two over there when I'm done," Dad said.

"Yay! Thank you, Daddy!" said Katie, clapping her hands.

Katie almost dragged her mom across the road and into the cute little Christmas store. They both gasped at the beautiful decorations all glittering and sparkling.

Katie gazed at all the ornaments – the snowmen, the snowballs, the snowflakes and the frosty looking icicles, long strands of clear beads that looked like drops of frozen water.

"Oh, Katie; look at this – for the top of the tree," Mom said.

Wow," Katie said, staring at the most beautiful tree ornament she had ever seen. "It's so *snowy*, Mom!"

It was a giant, clear, sparkling snowflake Christmas Tree topper that looked like it was made from ice.

Mom and Katie soon filled the basket to the brim with lots of new tree ornaments and decorations, and just as Mom was paying Grandma Christmas, Dad arrived back and poked his head in the door.

"I'm ready, ladies," Dad said, smiling at his girls.

Katie sat looking at her brand new tree ornaments all the way down the long country road back to the farm. She couldn't wait to get the tree set up in the house so she and Mom could start decorating it right away.

* * *

Dad set up the tree in the living room and they all stood back and admired it. It really was the perfect Christmas Tree.

"Our Snow Day tree is going to be the best Christmas Tree ever, Mom," Katie said.

"I agree!" said Mom. You start hanging the new ornaments and I'll go make some fresh popcorn for the garlands. And maybe I'll bring back some hot chocolate with me too!" Mom said.

"Yay!" said Katie.

"Marshmallows?" Mom asked.

"Duh!" said Katie, laughing.

Mom giggled and went off to the kitchen.

Katie was so into decorating the tree that she was paying no attention to anything else going on around her. Mom came back into the living room with a tray of hot chocolate, complete with lots of little mini marshmallows, and a big bowl of freshly popped popcorn for the garland.

"Katie! Look out the window!" Mom said.

Katie snapped her head around and looked outside.

"It's snowing!" she squealed.

"It's a blizzard out there!" said Mom. "We better run out and get those pine cones we wanted for the tree before they're all covered up with snow and we can't find them!"

"We better!" said Katie, rushing to the hall to put on her jacket, hat, scarf and gloves.

Katie had started the day so disappointed that the snow was a no show on Snow Day where she was. But not even half way through, it was turning into one of the best holiday days ever.

Not only did they have the best Christmas Tree in the whole world, with the prettiest, snowy decorations, she would be building a snowman and throwing snowballs before dinner, for sure! And even better, tomorrow would definitely be a Snow Day too!

Mom got a big basket out of the hall closet and the two of them went outside into the snowstorm and set about collecting pine cones to put the finishing touches on Katie's Snow Day Christmas Tree.

It was most definitely going to be the most beautiful snowy, icy, frosty Christmas Tree anyone had ever, ever seen, and the best Snow Day ever.

WAITING UP FOR SANTA

Mason wriggled restlessly under his bed covers and sighed.
Is it not morning yet? he thought to himself, the voice in his
head as grumpy as he was.

He got out of bed and crept along the hall, expertly avoiding
all the spots on the floorboards he knew creaked and groaned
when he stepped on them.

"Where d'you think you're going?"

He froze in his tracks and slowly turned around.

"I was firsty, mommy," he said to his mom.

"Uh-huh. Likely story, Mr. Mason Jr! I know where you were
going. You were going to wait up for Santa again, weren't you?"

He looked at her and tried his best to do those puppy-dog
eyes she always gave in to.

"Mason, you know you can't see him. He won't come in and
leave any presents for you if you stay up and try to see him. I
told you this last Christmas, honey," she said.

He didn't say anything because he didn't like lying. He always
felt bad when he lied to his mom or dad. And anyway, she knew
him so well he didn't even need tell her where he was going. She
already knew.

"Go on back to bed, sweetie. It won't be long until Santa gets
here and then you can open all your presents, OK?"

He did what he was told. Mom ruffled his hair on his way by
and followed him back to his bed. She tucked him in again and
kissed him on the forehead and yawned sleepily as she made her
way back to her own bedroom.

She hoped this would be his last attempt at seeing Santa. For
this year, at least.

* * *

He lay there awake still, wondering if she was asleep again
and if he could make another attempt at getting to the living
room without being discovered.

I gotta see him!

He took a deep breath as he went down the stairs passing by
the lush green garland of real cedar boughs that were strung
along the length of the handrail. They were covered in tiny,
sparkling white lights and shiny red artificial apples.

He smiled. He loved the smell of the cedar branches. They
were *so Christmassy.* Mom always made the house look so good
for the Holidays.

There were handmade wreaths she made herself on all the doors, decorated with big red or tartan ribbons and bows, and pine cones sprayed gold or covered in snowy white glitter. The Christmas tree was always so awesome – covered with white ornaments that looked like snowballs, brass bells and angels, shiny red baubles and masses of tiny white lights that looked like stars twinkling in the night sky.

I bet Santa loves our house!

He grinned at his thought and imagined Santa walking in and smiling at how *Christmassy* the house was.

And then the perfect hiding place came to him – right behind the Christmas tree.

That was it – perfect! He would wait for Santa, right here, behind the Christmas tree. That way, he would be sure not to miss him. That was the one place he could be absolutely sure Santa would head for, because he would need to leave all the presents there.

Mason climbed in behind the Christmas tree, being very careful not to step on the any of the gifts in the mountain already there. He sat hugging his knees in the cramped space smiling at all the presents around him. He loved Christmas so much.

And he began waiting for Santa.

It wasn't long before Mason's eyelids started to get heavy. He nodded off to sleep a few times but sat bolt upright, awake, and started watching again.

But soon, the twinkling of the lights and the sparkle of the glittered ornaments moving ever so gently soothed him back to sleep again.

The next time he woke up he didn't take up watching for Santa again. He yawned, a big loud, sleepyhead yawn and curled up in a ball under the Christmas tree and fell fast asleep.

* * *

"Merry Christmas, Mason!"

Mom and Dad cried out together as they burst into his room.

"Oh," Mom said.

"He's probably downstairs already, trying to figure out what's inside all the presents under the tree," Dad said.

John didn't care too much for Christmas. He thought it was a lot of expense for nothing. Both his parents thought the same. They had no room in their busy, stressful lives as high-powered business people for Christmas cheer or magic of any kind. John loved giving gifts to his wife and son, but he really didn't like

Christmas.

There was no sound coming from the living room, no noisy Christmas cartoons thundering from the TV, just the silent Christmas tree and the mountain of gifts that surrounded it.

John reached down behind a huge box to turn on the tree lights. He struggled to reach around it but made it.

"I'll check outside, honey; he's probably playing in the snow or something," Dad said. He had awakened in the middle of the night and noticed it was snowing heavily. He was sure Mason would be eager to get out there and make a snowman as soon as possible.

Mom chewed her bottom lip nervously. She ran around the house opening closets and checking the all the rooms.

There was no sign of him anywhere.

"Oh, John; where is he? What's happened to him?" Mom said, her voice a little shaky.

"I don't know, honey. Hey, wait a minute! Remember that time he climbed into the back of the SUV? He said he couldn't sleep though, because it wasn't the same when it wasn't going *vroom-vroom!* Remember that?" John smiled and gave a little laugh. Mason was a hoot and always brought a smile to his face.

Julia tried to smile back, but she was so worried about her little boy.

John wasn't smiling anymore when he came back from the garage. Mason wasn't in the back of the SUV. No sign of him in there either.

It seemed like he just disappeared into thin air.

Mom sat down on the sofa and hugged herself against the chill of the Christmas morning air that had rushed through the house when John opened the back door.

Her thoughts raced. She couldn't imagine where Mason could be.

There was no way somebody could have come into the house and taken him, and neither could he have left the house on his own – they would have heard the security system go off.

"John, he *has* to still be here in the house – the alarm – he wouldn't have been able to switch it off," she said.

"Oh. Actually, I forgot to set it last night, honey," John said.

Her heart sank. It was her one hope left that he was still nearby.

"We should call the police, right now. Let's not wait any longer. Every second counts with a lost child," Julia said.

"Just let me check the other rooms again, OK? Did you check under the beds and in the closets and all that?" he asked.

"I checked everywhere. He's not here," she said, her voice shaky.

But John was a little more calm than his wife. He knew that Mason was still in the house somewhere. He wouldn't wander off and run away.

John double checked all the rooms again and went outside. He even checked the storage shed at the far end of the garden.

Mom sat staring at the Christmas tree, her eyes beginning to fill with tears. She wanted to stay calm and not panic. Her gaze landed on a little pile of presents she hadn't wrapped.

The wrapping paper wasn't any she had bought. She picked one of them up and read the gift tag, thinking it was for her from her husband. She smiled. It said – *To Mason, no more waiting up to see me! Love, Santa.*

John came back; his face looked sad now.

"I guess it's time to call the police," he said, picking up the phone to dial 911.

Both of them looked at each other as they heard a noise coming from behind the Christmas tree.

"Was that a snore?" Dad asked.

The tree began to shake, the baubles bouncing up and down, swinging around, as Mason turned over in his sleep.

"Mason?" Mom called to him.

The tree shook again.

"Mommy?"

"Mason! Come here, you silly sausage!" she cried with delight.

Dad reached down behind the tree and pulled him up, hugged him and handed him over to Julia who squeezed him and covered him in little kisses.

She sat him down on his dad's knee.

"What on earth were you doing sleeping behind the Christmas tree?" Mom asked.

"I was waiting up for Santa," Mason said.

They both laughed.

"You know you can't see Santa, sweetheart," Mom said.

"Why not? I wanna see him!" Mason cried.

"Because if you see him then the magic will disappear and there will be no more Santa and then no more little boys and girls will get any presents at Chirstmas, forever!" Mom said.

"No fair!" Mason replied.

"I know, kiddo, but that's just how it is," Dad said. "You wouldn't want that to happen, now, would you?"

Mason suddenly sprang off his dad's knee and threw himself down in front of the tree.

"He came! He came! New pile!" Mason yelled at the top of his lungs.

"Oh, wow! Look Dad – Santa came!" Julia said and winked at John.

He smiled at her.

"That was a cute idea," she said to John in a whisper.

"What was?" John asked, his voice as quiet as hers.

"The stack of presents from Santa," she said.

"Huh?" John said, totally confused.

"Oh, come on. I know it was you. It wasn't me," she said.

She looked at him, studying his face. He looked as if he really *was* confused.

"I don't know what you're talking about, honey," John said.

"Sure, sure," she said, and winked at him again.

Mom went to the tree and started handing out presents. It was going to take a while just to sort them into piles for each of them.

John picked up one of the presents from the stack Mason was opening.

It was wrapped in unusual, very old fashioned looking paper that neither he nor Julia would pick. They both liked modern gift wrap – lots of metallic red and gold and sliver paper, or funky holographic ones. Julia certainly would *never* buy this gift wrap.

John looked at the gift tag. It wasn't Julia's writing and he knew he didn't buy the gifts or the wrapping paper.

He smiled at his wife and his little boy as they tore into their Christmas presents.

Maybe these are for us from Santa, even if we are grown ups! Maybe he thought we needed a little reminder of how lucky we all are, John thought to himself.

John made a start on the huge pile of Christmas presents in front of him, but preferred watching his wife and son open theirs to opening his own.

Mason handed Mom and Dad a present each from the pile of old fashioned-wrapped gifts.

"What's this?" Mom asked.

"They're for you! They got your names on," Mason said.

And he was right – the tags said *John* and *Julia*.

They both gasped as they tore into the wrapping paper and saw the gifts inside.

John stared at his wife, a look of surprise on his face and she mirrored his expression. They both knew that they had not bought these presents for each other.

"I don't believe it – I got one of these years and years ago when I was a little kid," John said, looking puzzled.

"And I got one of these when I was a little girl!" Julia said.

"Who from?" John asked.

"Santa!" she said.

"Me too," John said, smiling and frowning at the same time.

"How did you know..." Julia didn't even finish what she was going to say. There was no way John could have know she got one of these when she was a kid and there was no way she could have know John got that when he was a little boy either.

John smiled; he had a feeling that Santa's visit this year wasn't just for Mason. He knew in his heart that Santa wanted him to experience something he had never felt before, not even when he was a young boy - a little Christmas magic.

NO HO HO! MY ELVES ARE MISSING!

Santa was frantic. He ran around the toy factory like a headless chicken, opening doors and looking in rooms, checking in closets and under workbenches.

"No ho ho! My elves are missing! What am I going to do?" Santa cried.

It was true. There wasn't an elf to be seen anywhere. All of them, every last one, had disappeared.

He was in a panic now and yelled for Mrs. Claus.

"Goodness me! What ever is the matter, Chris?" Sandra Claus, Santa's wife asked, concerned. It wasn't like Santa to be so upset at all.

"All the elves are gone!" he said.

"Gone? What do you mean they're gone?" she asked, her turn to be alarmed now.

"I mean they're gone! As in they're not here. As in they've disappeared. I've turned the toy factory upside-down looking for them. I've looked in every room, behind every door, in every nook and cranny and under every workbench and table. They're not here. They're missing!" Santa said, his voice shaking.

He had no idea where they could have gone.

"Let's just go and check the toy factory again. It's huge. Maybe you missed something. Maybe they're just hiding and playing a trick on you," she said.

"They better not be, or they'll be working in shopping malls next Christmas, because I'm going to fire them all!" Santa said, angry at the thought they were playing a joke on him, and especially on Christmas Eve, their busiest and most stressful day of the whole year. But he knew in his heart that his beloved elves would never do such a thing.

That would be better than them all being missing though, he thought.

"Let's just go and see first, before you start thinking about firing anybody, OK?" Sandra said.

"OK," Santa said, trying to calm himself down.

They reached the toy factory again and started looking. Santa took the high places and Mrs. Claus took the low places. She checked under all the tables and benches. She checked all the low cupboards and closets and the lumber mill where the elves cut all the wood for the toys, and the sticky room where anything that needed sticking together got glued or nailed, and she checked the wrapping room too, where all the presents got wrapped and tied up in ribbons and bows.

"I don't get it, Chris. This is so strange! Where on earth did hundreds and hundreds of elves go all at once?" Mrs. Claus asked.

"If I knew that, Sandra, my dearest wife, we wouldn't be looking for them, would we?" Santa said, trying to smile at her. But the truth was, Santa was worried about his little helpers. Not only were they his workers, they were his friends too. They worked hard for him all year and sometimes he could be grumpy with them but they never, ever complained.

"Did you check the barn and the candy room?" Mrs. Claus asked.

"No, not yet. But I just came from the barn, so I know they're not there," Santa said.

"Oh, my goodness, Chris Kringle; what on earth are we going to do?" she asked.

"I don't know, Sandra. I really don't know," Santa said.
* * *
Santa and Sandra took different sides of the workshop and the house and went through them thoroughly. There wasn't so much as a pointy boot, or a stripey hat, or a jingle bell to be found. There was absolutely no sign that an elf had ever been here.

"Oh, no. What on earth has happened to my little friends?" asked Santa, tears welling up in his eyes. Where can they be? It's like they just disappeared into thin air. I don't understand it," he said, completely puzzled by the lack of elves around the place.

"Oh, dear. Oh, Chris. What if they were abducted by aliens?" Mrs. Claus said.

"Abducted by aliens? I don't think so, sweetheart. I think I would have noticed if a spaceship landed outside the toy factory and stole all my elves!" Santa said.

"Well, you are a teensy-weensy bit hard of hearing these days," Mrs. Claus said.

"Nonsense! I've got ears like a bat! I can hear the elves snoring clear across the other side of the yard in their house! I can hear snow falling on the roof in a hurricane! I can hear reindeer farting in the barn in the middle of the night!" Santa said.

"Chris Kringle! That's just a plain old lie!" Mrs. Claus said.

"Is not!" Santa said.

"Is too!" she said back.

"This is not helping me find my elves, Sandra," Santa said.

"I know. I'm sorry. But we've run out of places to look. They're just gone. Totally gone," she said.

"Oh, my giddy Aunt! Sandra! I just noticed something! They toys – they're all gone too!" Santa yelled.

"Oh, no! You mean you didn't load them already? I thought they were already in the sleigh, I didn't think anything of it," she said.

"No, they're not. All I did after we got up this morning was go to the barn and feed the reindeer. Then I went to the toy factory so we could start loading up. That's when I found they were gone," Santa said.

"When did you last see them?" she asked.

"Not since last night, before we all went to bed. They might have been gone all night for all I know," Santa said.

"What are we going to do? Christmas, Chris! The children! The presents!" Mrs. Claus cried.

"I know. I know. It doesn't look like there's going to be a Christmas this year, my dear. At least, not with presents." Santa said.

"This is terrible! Whoever did this has ruined Christmas for every single boy and girl in the whole world," she said.

Santa shook his head, in complete despair that he would not be able to deliver any presents to the children this year.

"Oh, no. Chris. You don't think it was..." Mrs. Claus almost asked but didn't finish what she was going to say.

"Yes, I do. I was afraid of this. I heard the other day that somebody cleaned out Easter Town of all their Easter eggs. And one of the elves told me he spoke to Cupid in Valentineville – they had all their hearts and flowers stolen too. You're right, Sandra. The Holiday Pirate stole our elves and all the toys!" Santa said.

"Oh, no. Oh, this is a nightmare! We have to get them back, Chris! We have to save Christmas!" Mrs. Claus said.

* * *

They called everybody they could think of. All the towns in Holiday World told them the same story – they had all been hit by the Holiday Pirate.

All the skeletons and tombstones and furry black spiders, all the pumpkins and gound-burster zombies had been stolen from Halloween Town.

All the American flags, and the red, white, and blue top hats, and the July 4th decorations in Independence City were all gone.

Even all the shamrocks ,and *Kiss Me – I'm Irish!* bowler hats, and the inflatable Leprechauns had been taken from St. Patrick Village too.

If they didn't get them all back, Santa knew, starting with Christmas, there would be no holidays anywhere in the world for a whole year.

"OK, let's start outside – see if we can follow the Holiday Pirate's tracks," Sandra said.

"Good idea!" Santa said and they both headed outside to begin the hunt for their missing elves and all the toys.

* * *

"Look! There's the big galoot's footprints! I'd know those great big huge feet anywhere!" Santa said.

"But they just end here. And look – just one set. None of these are the elves' footprints; they've got teeny tiny little feet," Mrs. Claus said.

"You know what this means, Sandra – it means they're still around here somewhere!" If they didn't go outside and they're not in the house or the barn or the toy factory..." Santa said, thinking where they could be around here.

"I know where they are! The Peppermint Mine!" said Mrs. Claus.

'That's it! They have to be there! Let's go! We're running out of time!" Santa yelled.

They ran to the barn and into Rudolph's stall that hid the secret trap door into the Peppermint Mine where teams of elves mined peppermint candies and candy canes.

They opened it and immediately all the elves cheered and began to run out of the mine.

"Santa! Thank goodness!" cried Eddie the Head Elf. "We have to save Christmas!"

"Thank Heaven you're all OK! We were so worried about you," Mrs. Claus said.

"We're fine, Sandra! But the bandit got away! There was nothing we could do. He had some sort of new weapon he used against us, were powerless to stop him – that's how he managed to steal every single toy in the whole factory too!" Eddie said.

"A weapon?" Santa said.

"Yes! It picks things up! He pointed it at us and we all flew up into the air and we were carried to the Peppermint Mine. All he had to do was open the trap door and close it behind us. I don't even know how he knew where the mine was, Santa. He must have been spying on us!" Eddie said.

"Oooh, that pesky pirate!" Mrs. Claus said, and stomped her foot in anger.

"OK, we know where he lives and we have to go right now if we're going to make it in time to load the sleigh and deliver the presents," said Santa.

"Let's go! We've got to save Christmas!" yelled Eddie to the elves. They all cheered and followed Santa.

"We'll have to take the sleigh. It's the only thing fast enough," said Santa, harnessing up the reindeer for the ride.

    *   *   *

Santa and a few of the elves took off and headed for the lair of the Holiday Pirate. It was snowing a blizzard of gigantic snowflakes and the wind howled around them. They could hardly see anything, the snow was so thick, everything covered in a pure white blanket.

The elves shivered with the cold but they had to get through this – they had Christmas to save for all the girls and boys all across the world who were sleeping soundly in their beds, waiting for Christmas to arrive.

"Santa couldn't see to guide the sleigh, but he knew that Rudolph knew the way to the pirate's home.

They rode on, teeth chattering in the freezing air that surrounded them. The reindeer flew fast and in just a few minutes they had arrived.

"There!" Eddie the Head Elf pointed. "There it is! I can see the skull and crossbones on his roof!"

"Yes! That's it!" Santa said, taking the sleigh down gently in the snowstorm and landing outside the Holiday Pirate's front door.

Santa knocked on the big black door of the house. There was no answer.

He pushed the doorbell – it was in the shape of a skull and when he pushed the button its eyes glowed red and it gave off a piercing scream instead of a *ding-dong*.

Still no answer.

"Eddie, open that lock-up door if you can – the presents must be in there," Santa said.

Eddie struggled with the lock but managed to open the door. And there they were – all the missing presents.

"Hold it right there, Santa!" the Holiday Pirate roared.

"You!" yelled Santa. "You mean, nasty, horrible, despicable, evil..." Santa said.

"You say the nicest things, Santa," the pirate said.

"Why did you do this? Why would you want to ruin Christmas for every boy and girl in the whole world?" Santa asked him.

"Because I can. Because I hate the Holidays! Because everybody is always mean to me!" the pirate said.

"Everybody is always mean to you because you're always stealing the Holidays!" Santa said.

"Nobody likes you because you do bad things all the time. You stole Christmas!" Eddie hollered at the thief.

"Come on, Chris! You better get going! You're about an hour late in leaving!" Eddie said.

"We'll deal with you later, Holiday Pirate. You're not getting away with this! We're going to see that you get punished for what you've done. You just can't go around Holiday World taking what you want! The Holidays are for everybody to enjoy," Mrs. Claus said. She was very angry at the Holiday Pirate. He just took what he wanted without asking, and didn't care how it effected anybody else. He was selfish and only cared about himself.

Santa and Mrs. Claus would make sure the Sheriff of Holiday World came and arrested him after the Holidays. But right now, Santa and his elves had a lot of work to do.

* * *

They rushed back to the house and Santa threw on his famous red and white suit and hat and headed back to his sleigh. He always took a few elves, including Eddie, with him to keep everything organized, so he didn't leave a baby doll in a pink dress for a boy who wanted a skateboard with a skull and crossbones on it. Santa couldn't do it all on his own – he was so glad to have his elf helpers back – without them there would be no Christmas any year, not just when the Holiday Pirate stole it!

But he was glad to have them back because they were his friends to and he loved them all.

* * *

Santa delivered all the presents on time, with a lot of help from his elf friends. Christmas was saved and all the little boys and little girls all around the world had no idea how close they had come to not having a Christmas at all. But they would never know, as they sat and opened their presents on Christmas morning, that the Holiday Pirate almost ruined it for the whole world, or that Santa, Mrs. Claus and their awesome elves and reindeer, saved Christmas that year for all of us.

MERRY CHRISTMAS, EVERYONE!

Watch out for the Holiday Pirate!

With love from Holly-Anne

x   x   x

If you loved these cute family Christmas stories and would like to share them with everybody on your social networks, or your own blog or website, you can point them to Holly-Anne's Blog.

You can stop by there and say 'hello' too! Holly-Anne would love to hear from you!

HOLLY JOLLY FAMILY BLOG!
for Christmas poems, Holiday crafts, movie reviews, and all sorts of festive fun!

http://KidsChristmasStories.Blogspot.com